Smooth
A Novel of Horror

catt dahman

Copyright.
catt dahman
© 2014, catt dahman

ALL RIGHTS RESERVED. This book contains material protected under International and Federal Copyright Laws and Treaties. Any unauthorized reprint or use of this material is prohibited. No part of this book, including the cover and photos, may be reproduced or transmitted in any form or by any means, electronic or mechanical, including photocopying, recording, or by any information storage and retrieval system without express written permission from the author / publisher. All rights reserved.
The characters, places, and events depicted are fictional and do not represent anyone living or dead. This is a work of fiction.

Part One

Chapter 1

Pax and Katie walked across the park together, beneath the sweeping oaks and fragrant pines, enjoying for a few seconds the banishment of the blistering hot sun. The shade was dark enough so that it felt like walking into a tall cave, cool and fragrant, and it cut off most of the far-away noises. Pax sat down on a bench and took off his backpack with a sigh of relief.

Katie lifted the front of her body up onto the bench so she was almost face-to-face with Pax. Her eyes reminded him that she was being a good girl but that he could hurry up and do his job. She needed something now and was patient, but mindful of his responses.

"Okay. I *am* hurrying. I know...you'd do it yourself, but the lack of opposable thumb issue is causing the...I know...I know...."'"

He reached for her collar and first unclamped a D bracket which went on a D clip on her collar that ran through a hole bored through her 'quick-fix', small, clean, metal water dish. He set it onto the bench and unclipped the second D ring and took a little insulated tubular bag from her neck, and from that, a bottle of water. Pax poured the water into the bowl and set in on the ground.

Katie watched Pax with her head cocked and waited patiently and politely until he had unhooked his own canteen and uncapped it. When he started sipping at his water, Katie began to lap her own water. It was difficult to wait.

Pax handed her a small beef stick; she ate the stick, and then they shared three more with a few cubes of cheese, five small crackers, and three ginger cookies each. Next, they drank more water. Katie looked at him, letting him know she was game to eat more snacks, especially cheese, but he didn't offer any more. At least he hadn't tried to offer her any more of the other stuff in a baggie; she didn't like trail mix at all.

Afterwards, Pax washed the bowl out for Katie, thoroughly dried it, and refilled her bottle and his canteen. He clipped his canteen back on; then, he fastened her bowl and water bottle back to her collar and to the straps that made them her little back pack. She also wore a bright green bandana around her neck. She was accustomed to carrying her gear for herself and ignored the faint tinny noises all of it made as she ran.

"Let's have our rest," Pax said. Katie lay next to the bench in the soft leaves. For this, she gave in because she wasn't tired, but if he wanted to nap, then she would pretend to as well.

Cold Springs Est. March 12, 1929

Pax read the sign a few times as he sat on the bench. Katie opened one eye and knew his words mattered not to her. Unless it was about cheese, the sign was uninteresting.

It was an old town, full of idiosyncrasies and secrets, ripe for the telling and was a self-contained place here in the middle of nowhere. That idea had its charms. It wasn't as if he had to read the sign so many times, but he kept wondering what the place had looked like back then. How did people know where to set up towns? Did the original settlers stay?

What did the trees know? Had they wondered about the newcomers? Most of the original people were gone now, but the trees still grew. Pax always wondered about the past and wished he could see pictures of everything, before and now.

In a few minutes, he stood, and Katie jumped to chase the red ball he tossed for her, leaping into the air to catch it or using her nose to dig it up from the leaves that the ball stirred up.

He threw it over and over. She scrambled on the walk way and then caught it on a bounce. Pax put the ball away when they were both winded.

"Good job, Katie. Give me a shake."

She shook his hand.

"Give me a kiss."

She gave him a sloppy lick.

"Who is the best Katie?"

She woofed happily.

Pax motioned her to come along side him. "Okay, let's go check out this Cold Springs. Be on your best behavior."

"Woof," she replied.

"I will, too," Pax said conversationally. {It was better to talk to his dog than to talk to the voices in his head, if he had any.} He felt dogs were great conversationalists. They listened, didn't comment overly much, and told no secrets.

He adjusted a strap on his backpack and settled into the same timing he had maintained across two states when he didn't have a ride. It was a determined pace and one that would get them places, but it wasn't so hurried that they missed seeing anything interesting along the way.

As they walked over a bridge that crossed a wide little river branch, Pax glanced down into the water and found it clear and deep, running fast over big rocks and shaded by huge trees that dotted the sandy bank. He looked out at the branch of water and wondered how a photo might look taken of Katie and him standing there on the old bridge; he thought it would be a good picture of the bridge and his canine traveler.

It would be a good photo of him since the long walk had toned and trimmed him quite a bit. He was back in shape and leaner than normal. The walk had been good for him in many ways. Months before, he hadn't the strength and endurance he had now. His slight paunch was gone, and his belly was flat.

Had there been a picture taken, it would have been of the man and dog, looking out across the water on the low bridge that flooded occasionally but had served as the town's only entryway for more than a century. Cold Springs butted up to jagged hills and farmer's fields, and the roads ended where those farms began.

The bridge was constructed of concrete, rock, and brown bricks and was mossy along the edges of the opening arch the water ran through. A strong wooden railing and slats were along the sides, and above, was a wide area for walkers and two lanes for traffic, and all were covered with a thin layer of cracked and pitted cement.

If there had been a picture, the bridge would have looked the same a decade before, a day before; there would be no real changes. The difference in scenery would have been just the man and the dog.

The man, Pax, wore a clean white tee shirt with a faded, but clean, buttoned up checked shirt, a loose pair of faded-almost-white jeans and heavy, expensive hiking boots. The jeans had been snug two months before, and the boots had been unscuffed. Those things had changed.

Anyone looking would have noticed he was clean cut for a drifter, too relaxed for a common hitchhiker, and too focused for anyone who was simply looking for a new town to call home. From a distance, Pax would be difficult to describe with any details.

He was of average weight, had no facial hair, and his plain, brown hair was cut short. With a trim body and longish legs, he was forgettable except for his pale, sky-blue eyes and the big grin he almost always wore. Only one who was close enough to see his eyes and the grin would describe him accurately.

With the pale eyes and infectious grin, he was the type that became better looking as people were around him. It wasn't just personality; with familiarity came a relaxation of his features that made him attractive. It wasn't anything he thought about, however.

His dog was by far more interesting to him.

Katie wore her little backpack and the green bandana against her black fur; she never complained about carrying her own gear. She was pure muscle since she was a youngish dog, but she was still old enough to be well behaved and to walk happily and politely beside her master and friend.

She was beautiful, well behaved, and smart.

Before each ride they had accepted when they were hitchhiking on the main roads and highways, she had sniffed the cars and trucks thoroughly and indicated she thought it was a safe ride free of drugs or alcohol or anything nefarious. She might not have known thumbing rides was dangerous {And it was very dangerous}, but she knew whose cars smelled bad and whose smelled safe.

Only once on a dreary evening when Pax had thought a man seemed fine to ride with, had she whined and cast him a nervous look.

He didn't know what she had scented, but he took her

advice and said to the driver, "Never mind", and they walked, Pax wondering what it was Katie knew and he didn't. And whether or not it had been a dangerous ride, Pax didn't know, but everyone they rode with, all those who Katie had okayed, were generous, friendly, safe drivers who might grudgingly accept gasoline money but always shared meals and wasted away the miles with happy chatter. Everyone had been particularly taken with Katie and her excellent manners.

Katie might have been wrong, or maybe the man had an unusual scent that confused her, and Pax would never know what it had been, if anything. He never saw anything about the man in newspapers, but something had bothered Katie. It was better to be safe than to take his chances and hope he could survive, if threatened.

Miles had flown by.

They had met fascinating people, people with stories, and some with few words at all. In each, Pax had found a slice of life; it was as if he could, for a few minutes, see into another life.

The trek had also afforded Pax the chance to kick at pebbles and see what was tossed out onto the side of highways. He had even picked up a silver ring set with a pretty black faceted stone (Okay, it could be a black diamond but was likely a cheap stone instead} and countless pennies and nickels. Dirty diapers and toilet tissue, he skirted.

Some items made no sense. He wondered why there was always just one shoe. Never two. At those times, he felt locked out of stories and was curious.

It wasn't safe, maybe, but it was how Pax had wanted to travel to Cold Springs, with just the necessities and his best friend, Katie, and cash strapped to his leg and nothing remaining of his material possessions once he had sold or given them all away. He felt freer and more with the world than he ever had before with nothing tying him down such as a car or a house or a job. {He was a hobo at heart}.

He had made a great deal of cash selling clutter he didn't want or need and found a certain catharsis in having everything that mattered in his backpack or walking beside of him. The church had been thrilled with his donation of everything that hadn't sold; he took pride in knowing that his cast offs would clothe people in need. But this wasn't just altruistic; he had just wanted to be free of material goods and have the money to start over somewhere else if he desired.

Somewhere such as Cold Springs.

Maybe.

"It's beautiful here, isn't it?" Pax asked.

Katie woofed in agreement, it seemed. {She might have also been looking at a squirrel}. She panted and showed her doggy grin as she danced around him to get him moving again. There was so much to smell and see.

As he looked out, refusing to budge yet, she leaned into him impatiently until her weight finally made him take a step and stop staring at the scenery. "Fine. You can have your way," he said as he began walking again, crossing the old bridge, and emerging on the main drag through the town.

Chapter 2

It was like walking into a stage set of a television show from the 1950s with the old, brick buildings which were orderly and neat, charming street lights, and shops of every kind. The town was welcoming and safe.

"There you have a mechanic's shop, and it's a gas station. They and the one up the street are very competitive. That old building is a florist...that is flowers, Katie...and antiques and next to it...a bank. There is a small hotel, and beside it is a spa. Tourists come here in droves. Did you know they have both a hot and cold natural spring here? They have mud baths there you would love and massages; those are like getting scratched and petted, only it's for people."

The small area for parking was packed because people came from other places to visit this spa. "The owner grows some of her own herbs for this spa, and she grows some other herbs for herself to smoke, if ya catch my drift," he talked to Katie as they walked. {The woman smoked a lot from what Pax had been told}.

Katie peed on a tree.

"Katie, stop peeing on trees; that's rude."

Pax knew a lot of little details about this place that most who visited would never have guessed; he wasn't psychic, but rather, he had been told these snippets. "That gas station? The prices will rise and fall all week as they compete with the place at the end of this street. And at the bank, the president's wife is bald as a new baby, but she wears expensive wigs she orders from somewhere in France, and she thinks people don't know, but they do."

Katie sniffed at a stop sign and waited for Pax to indicate they could cross the street and carry on. She knew at places like this she was to wait until he said it was okay to go on. She didn't want to get smushed by a car. She waited, listening, in case he might mention the cheese again.

"The school is that way, tiny with less than a hundred school children and a handful of teachers. Most of the graduates marry local and stay here, and could I tell you stories about the goings on with all those people...." He trailed off. "Here you have good kids from good families, but Katie, there are secrets in any town and the ideas here are no better or worse than in the city. People are people...."

There were a newspaper/electronics/ office-needs building, an antiques shop, and a shop called a Five and Dime which meant it was cheaper than going into the city, and it was clever, but merchandise was certainly not a nickel or a dime in cost.

"Pharmacy there, always count your pills because a few are always missing, accidentally, of course," said Pax as he chuckled. "Barbecue there, it isn't great, but it's okay; the cook is always trying to make his recipe better." He admired the details on the big courthouse building behind the pharmacy and barbecue place, at least those he could see.

When Pax saw the building he was looking for, he grinned again. It was on a corner and large, an eatery named Coral's Diner that sat across from a farmer's market, where everyone bought vegetables and fruit. {No pesticides or chemicals used, they claimed}.

Although he didn't see it, he knew that the back parking lot of Coral's was full and that the diner at this hour would be packed with patrons, feasting on the delicious food, drinking good, strong coffee or iced jasmine tea, and chattering about the day they had. There would be families and couples, lone diners, teens, and the old folks, and the music playing would be old country such as Jim Reeves, Conway Twitty, Patsy Cline, and Johnny Cash.

Pax hummed a little. Katie liked when he did.

There would be specials at the diner such as crispy chicken fried steak, smothered in thick or creamy gravy, meatloaf with a tomato and pepper glaze, or fat, juicy hamburgers with thick, home fries, of course. The vegetables for the side dishes came fresh from the farmer's market across the road: corn and beans and squash.

A spaghetti dinner with bread or broiled, savory pork chops served with fresh carrots and big salads was offered. A vegetable and beef stew and a soup of green beans, cabbage, potatoes, and ham were popular. The rolls and corn bread were homemade, slathered with sweet butter.

The waitresses might offer the pinto beans, turnip greens, and a tall glass of buttermilk with cornbread, too, all you could eat as a special. Pax's mouth began to water as he thought about the menu.

Coral, the owner, was the cook, and he always came up with spicy sauces and was prone to adding an extra side to the orders so patrons could really fill up on his good food. He even made his own pickles, so along with pickled cucumbers, he pickled other things such as peppers and onions and carrot sticks.

"I could do with a few pickles. That sounds good, huh? No? You have no taste, Katie."

Katie looked indignant as Pax put a leash on her and clipped it to a bicycle rack, but she sat down in the shade and sighed. She could smell the food. What insanity was this? To keep her out here when the good stuff was inside? Maybe it was a test to see if she was a good girl; she was.

"This will just be for a little while, and I'll bring back dinner for you, okay? I don't want you running off on me."

She refused to make eye contact. She hadn't planned to run away, and this was insult to injury. She might have gone to play with squirrels, but this was unjust.

Pax went into the diner where the wonderful scents of food assaulted him, teasing his taste buds while the chatter filled his ears. Several stools were unoccupied at the snack bar, so he sat down and waited for the waitress, Lydia, to come take his order. She was blonde, thirty, but she claimed to be twenty-seven. She chomped gum habitually and wore a tight, short, royal blue dress with red piping with her high-topped sneakers. She was a cute gal.

"Howdy, stranger, and welcome to Coral's. Can I get you a menu, or do you have an idea what ya want? Now Coral can make ya anything you got a hankerin' for, but the specials are mighty delicious."

"Hi, Lydia," he said as he glanced at her name tag, "I want a Coral's double cheese burger with the works, and give me a side of chili fries and a glass of iced tea, please."

"Good choice although anything is a good choice here. Chili

fries are delish. And how do ya want that beef patty cooked?"

"Make it rare. And then on the side, I'll have two doubles of meat and cheese for my dog out there."

She strained to see. "Awe, that black one. He or she?"

"She. That's Katie."

"Ya want that tea sweet?"

"No, unsweetened, please."

"Coming right up," she said as she tore off the top sheet of the pad and slid it through to the cook in the back.

That would be Coral. Pax watched him, and he was a little star-struck.

"Pretty busy," Pax noted, as expected, as he looked around at the memorabilia and posters of the New England Patriots. All the seats were in royal blue, and here and there were accents of red against the stainless steel tables and counter.

"Always is. You just passing through or going to the spa or what?" She giggled fetchingly as he didn't look the spa type.

"Enjoying the town," he said, only fibbing a little since it wasn't a lie but just that he was holding back information.

"Staying long?" she asked and smiled prettily. She was curious.

"Depends on how things go, I suppose."

Lydia slid a little metal rack close to him that was filled with ketchup, hot sauce, a jar of home made spiced pickles, Coral's own steak sauce, salt and pepper, and sweetener for the tea. She handed him a rolled napkin of cutlery and a stack of napkins. "You'll need them for the burger; it's juicy and messy." She gave him a cute, flirty wink.

She waited on other patrons, and Pax watched people around him as they dined. As soon as a table was empty and cleaned, a new couple or a family was waiting to sit and eat dinner. The diner was as clean and neat as he knew it would be, was tastefully decorated with just the right amount of color and big screened televisions, and the waitresses all smiled and looked good in their uniforms. It was a place that a couple could enjoy for a date before a movie or a family would like to eat lunch after Sunday service, and where a lone diner didn't feel alienated and stared at for being alone.

It wasn't fancy, but it was the cleanest diner Pax had ever been in, with everything in good repair and gleaming. The waitresses didn't have that washed out look some got as they followed a set routine, but all were cheerful and energetic. It was just as he had known it would be.

When his order came, the extra burgers were on a separate paper plate with a big helping of meaty chili on top. "Katie deserves it," Lydia said.

Pax thanked her. He slipped outside and gave Katie her dinner, waited for her woof to say *'thank you'* and then returned to his spot at the counter to survey the huge burger: two thick meat patties cooked just right; two big slices of cheese; purple, sweet onions, lightly warmed; fresh green lettuce; several slices of salted and peppered deep red tomatoes; crisp pickles chopped to bits; and homemade jalapenos that peeked from the toasted buns. A third slice of cheese nestled between the meat patties, and the burger dripped with tangy secret sauce and thick slabs of crunchy bacon that hung out the sides.

For a second, Pax wanted to hang on to the aroma and savor it. As good as it would taste, the anticipation was good, too.

Pax opened wide and bit into the burger, sighing as he chewed; it was delicious. The chili fries were thick wedges, fried to perfection and then loaded with homemade chili with a little kick to it, and lightly covered with cheese. He cooled his mouth with gulps of tea. The flavors almost were an over-load. Everything was perfect.

Lydia returned, refilled his glass, and smiling asked, "Good?"

"Fantastic." Pax wiped his chin and grinned back.

"All the veggies are from the farmer's market across the street. Save room for dessert," she suggested as she refilled more glasses.

Savoring each bite, he looked around at all of the activity. He watched one particular waitress more than anyone else, seeing her smile and greet people by name and serving the good food with pride. Her hair, braided down her back, was almost black, and her eyes were greenish hazel; she was dressed in the same kind of royal blue uniform as the other waitresses, but she wore a pair of hiking boots with the outfit, unusual but sexy in some way.

He ate every bite of the burger and the fries and even the carrot sticks that decorated the plate; they were tangy with a garlic flavor. He was stuffed but wanted more.

"Now what kind of dessert sounds good to you?" Lydia asked.

"I'm getting too full. But I'd take some more tea," Pax said. As she poured, he shrugged in a casual manner and asked, "That waitress there, is her name Annie?"

Lydia frowned. "That's Annette or Annie."

Pax realized that the other woman's name tag must say Annette, and he had used her informal name. "She looks almost as capable as you are."

Lydia broke into her grin again, popping her gum and replied, "Mister, you are a sweet talker."

"Nah. Not me. She caught my eye," and then he added, "too".

"Oh, yeh?"

Pax waited a second. He knew Lydia had a boyfriend that owned and worked at the mechanic shop. His name was Chris; he had long hair and a beard and liked to ride his Harley. Lydia might be a little flirty, but she was devoted to the guy who treated her like a queen. "So?"

Lydia leaned on the counter in order to speak quietly. "She's single all right, but she has this man she likes on the Internet, if you can imagine; they talk all the time. I'd say she's pretty well taken."

"Oh," said Pax looked down, "Taken."

"You betcha."

"Internet, huh? And she likes him?"

"She's crazy for him, but he lives far away. But they talk every night, and she's nuts for him. He has a funny name, too, Pax." She wiped the counter, concentrating on a spot of ketchup.

Pax held out a hand, "Nice to meet you, Lydia. And it isn't so funny, short for Paxton."

Jaw dropped, she shook his hand and then covered her

mouth as she began to giggle madly. "She said he...uh...you were going on a trip, and she's been mooning over not chatting. What are you *doing* here?" Her tone was as if she had known him for years. She appraised him more carefully, finding him average but with a wonderful grin, and those baby blues would knock a gal's panties off. "She is gonna go nuts over you, handsome."

"I came to meet Annie. Shhhh, I wanna surprise her, so don't you tell. Now, you're being a sweet talker."

Lydia giggled again. "All this way to meet Annie. Wow, just wow. She's gonna pop a cork."

"Would you ask her to come over; tell her there's a problem and that I need to speak with her? I want to surprise her. Do you think she'd like that?"

Lydia nodded and answered, "Oh, she's gonna be surprised all right, big time, Hon."

Outside, the harsh sunlight faded as clouds moved in suddenly. Distantly, they could hear thunder, which made all of the customers stop talking for a fraction of a second, and then they went back and carried on, maybe discussing the weather. If it rained, Pax was glad he had reached his destination and would not be out in the bad weather.

Lydia spoke to Annie in a whisper, and Annie glanced at Pax. She looked a little perplexed as if she knew him and couldn't place him, but she finished cleaning a table, handed the container to Lydia, and walked over. "Yes, sir, how can I help you today?"

He looked like pictures she had seen, but he was not in a place he was expected to be in, so Annie was obviously having an itch in her brain but was unsure how she knew this man. It made him grin harder.

"The burger was outstanding."

"Glad to hear it," she said.

"And the home fries and chili were superb."

"Good."

Pax pretended to think hard, "But now this is the problem: I can't believe the famous Coral Robbins, former linebacker for the Pats, is a cook in the diner...." He paused. "*It defies logic.*"

He had used those exact words often to her as they sent

messages back and forth across states, teasing her, and her face showed she was flummoxed, trying to figure out how this stranger was using the exact words he had used. He could almost see her mind grabbing to make sense of this.

"You wouldn't know *logic* if it bit you in the ass," she said automatically, just as she had typed the words many times.

"Biting ass seems a bit *violent*," he responded as he always did.

Like Lydia, Annie's mouth dropped open as she understood. "Oh, my God, Pax? Pax? My hair is a mess." She started smoothing it back, embarrassed and excited. Her nerves jumped. She turned pink and looked suddenly a little shy and nervous. Her heartbeat raced.

"In the flesh."

"I...well...oh my, Pax?" She was about to jump out of her skin because she was so thrilled to see him.

He realized with a thud in his belly that this was an important moment: either she'd be disappointed and he had come a long way for nothing, or the magic was real, and she'd be as excited to see him as he was to see her.

"Oh, you crazy man!" She ran around the counter and grabbed him into a hug. It was a real hug, too, not one of those polite, pretend hugs that women sometimes gave with more patting than hugging. She squeezed him tightly.

He smelled the scent of food she had served and underneath, a lemony fragrance of her shampoo and clean skin. She felt sturdy, not too thin, and very warm in his arms; he hated when she pulled away to look at him to ask, "What are you doing here in Cold Springs?"

"Ummm, going to the spa?"

"You are not." She laughed, eyes twinkling. "You came all this way to meet me, really? Are you really here? Pax, I can't believe this."

"Yup. Sold my truck, hitched and walked, and here I am to meet the toughest, prettiest girl playing *Mafia Kings* on the Internet. I always said I would do something stupid and crazy one day because of you."

"And you did. But I am not gonna scold you for the biggest surprise of my life," Annie said as she blushed, slicked her hair back and wished she had put on lipstick or something. She wasn't ready to meet Pax when she looked this disheveled. And my, wasn't he an attractive man, just like his pictures? Had she been paying attention, she would have known it was him sitting there or at least thought it was his doppelganger.

She knew he was cute in his pictures, but he was handsome. His blue eyes crinkled at the edges, and he looked at her as if he were taking her in all at once, seeing her every nuance. She felt self-conscious for a second, and then it faded as she fell into their comfortable friendship. This was the Pax she had come to know from exchanged e-mails and pictures, *Mafia King* gaming, and messaging.

"So, did I screw up royally by coming here uninvited?"

Annie laughed. "No way! I am excited to meet you finally, but you could have picked a time when I was fancied up."

"You look great."

"So do you." Thunder almost drowned out her words.

"Katie is out there."

"Outside?" she asked. "I can't wait to meet her. Oh, tell you what. Bring her around back, and she can go into the lounge so she won't get soaked."

"You sure it's okay?" He wanted to ask if it were okay that he was here to meet her and was he putting Annie on the spot.

"Positive."

Pax finally dragged his eyes away from her and got Katie, who was dancing with nervousness over the approaching storm. They walked around to the back of the diner. Thick dark clouds were rolling in quickly with flashes of lightning and ear-splitting booms of thunder. For a second or two, Pax watched the clouds, feeling a bit concerned for some reason. But he shook off the weird feeling, attributing it to the excitement over meeting Annie and hurried to the open door where he and Katie went inside.

Off a hall was a restroom for staff and across from it, were a clean but plain lounge with a tattered plaid sofa, a big television, and a few chairs and tables with a sink and counter covered by a min-fridge and microwave. Pax snickered to see the conveniences even in the lounge.

Katie sniffed around quickly and then greeted Annie with a 'woof' and a sloppy kiss; Annie hugged her tightly. "She's beautiful," Annie said. "She looks just like her pictures. So do you." Annie's cheeks turned pink again.

"Very beautiful," Pax agreed although he was unsure which one of the females he meant. Annie's blush made him fairly certain that it was she whom he had been looking at when he said that, and she probably knew it.

Katie nosed around a little more and then settled into a corner, curled up, and fell asleep almost at once. She was full as a tick and comfortable, glad to be out of the approaching rain.

Pax smiled, "I got her two doubles with cheese, and Lydia added chili; she's full and happy thanks to Coral's cooking and Lydia's idea to add the chili."

Annie knelt to unhook Katie's water dish and then filled it at a sink in the little room and set it next to Katie.

"I am so surprised by this; it's so good to finally meet you for real. I'm glad you pulled this insane, wicked trick on me. Will you stay a while so we can talk in person?" She cocked her head prettily.

"If you want me to, I'll stay as long as I'm welcome, okay?"

"Come out front and sit; I'll sneak over and visit; I am off at seven tonight."

"That's a deal." Pax followed her after dropping his backpack.

"Coral, hey, Coral, guess what? The man I am always talkin' to on the computer, well here he is," said Annie as she motioned Pax to the cooking line.

Coral Robbins was a big man, wide and tall and heavily muscled. Stripping off his gloves, the giant came over to shake hands. "I didn't know you were coming here."

"He surprised me. I didn't know either, but here he is," Annie said. "Pax...Coral; Coral...Pax."

The two men studied one another after the handshake. Coral asked the usual questions about how Pax had gotten there, how long he was staying, and why he had suddenly come to Cold Springs, and then he muttered, "If you hurt my gal, I'll break your legs."

"Coral!" Annie blushed again.

Pax looked at the dark-skinned, African American, former defensive end whom he and hundreds of thousands had idolized during the man's career, judged the other man's strength and speed and decided that they would be evenly matched for a while as Pax was no slouch. He then told himself the big man could indeed break his legs if he wished to, probably several times over. "Yes, Sir, I don't aim to hurt her at all; I'm right fond of her."

"And you came all this way to surprise her?"

"I can't believe it," Annie said.

Coral rubbed his jaw in thought, taking in all the information and wondering how he could make sure this fellow wouldn't hurt a good girl like Annie. His eyes lit up. "You know anything about cooking? My other cook is off today with his wife having a baby, and I am short-handed. Seems you could cut fries and smear mayonnaise on a bun, if nothing else."

Annie rolled her eyes. "Seriously?"

"I am a desperate man, Annie Jo."

Pax knew she hated her middle name and couldn't suppress a grin. "I think I could even handle a grilled cheese sandwich if I tried real hard to figure out what all goes into one."

"Ha, ha, okay, come on and get into an apron and get your hands clean. Annie...."

"I know, go tend the customers. Slave driver, cruel and wicked boss, evil overseer of...."

"Get gone," Coral ordered with a pearly white smile that reached his eyes. After she skipped out of the room with a smile and a half-wave, Coral told Pax, "I have questions about your intentions, and if you're working, I can get more information 'cause I won't give you time to lie; I'll keep you too busy."

"*Quid pro quo.* You ask my intentions, and I get to ask you NFL secrets."

"You drive a mean bargain. It's a deal." Coral said as he threw a snowy-white apron at Pax who caught it and tied in on.

Chapter 3

For the next few hours, Pax did much more than make a few sandwiches as Coral went on about how he made each dish, what he put into recipes, how much spice he added, and how long each item had to cook. In between the demonstrations, Coral asked Pax questions, and Pax answered, only faintly aware that he wasn't getting as many questions answered in return as Coral taught him to cook, lulling him with interesting culinary tricks.

Coral had a certain way about him. He moved easily, but fast, and the whole time, he talked about this and that, tossing in occasional questions, but always with one eye on his task and one on Pax. He was direct, but he also relied on his instincts and probed a little at a time. He was pleased that Pax just talked, never launching into a speech, but just chatted, sometimes saying something about Annie or him in the same sentence as he mentioned adding turmeric to the simmering chili.

Annie periodically came back to check on them, to either make sure Pax hadn't run away or that Coral hadn't broken his legs or maybe just to reassure herself that Pax was, indeed, really in Cold Springs. Each time, she gave Pax a smile that made him feel warm.

"She likes you," Coral noted.

"I hope she does. I like her. A lot."

"You sticking around a while?" Coral asked as he smothered a perfectly cooked, tender chicken fried steak with thick milk-gravy and motioned Pax to add the creamed potatoes and green beans on the side. Pax slid a big hand-made roll onto the plate and a piece of parsley as he had been shown. Then as instructed, he added some crisp, tangy, hot pickles from a jar. "Those pickles, they have some lime juice, garlic, and pepper so that the citrus and heat cleanses the palate. They make the dish real."

"Ahhh. Makes sense," Pax smirked. "I'd like to stick around. I'll stay until she wants me to go, I reckon. She might get tired of me. I like the way those taste. The garlic is just right."

"Need a job?"

"You offering me one?"

"I'm offering so I can keep an eye on you and so my other cook can spend some time with the new mama and baby. You aren't too dumb to follow my expert instructions, it seems."

Pax laughed. "Smartest cook in the kitchen, I betcha. I'll take the job."

"I pay fairly well 'cause we do a damned fine business here, won't get rich, but it's honest, and you'll do fine with the pay around here. And your co-workers are tops."

"I believe that. Annie always talked about you being a fair boss."

"I expect my employees to be punctual and personally clean, and in the diner, they keep things very clean, are friendly, and enjoy the work, or they get out. Sound fair?"

Pax nodded. "Very. My dog is in the lounge."

For some reason that made Coral laugh until he cried. He stopped and wiped his face, and Pax laughed with him. It was a few minutes before Coral could talk without howling again with laughter. "Okay. Well, as long as it behaves, I can live with that." He loaded a plate with huge slices of meatloaf, drizzling a chunky tomato glaze over it. "Corn and Taters, slide them a bit of that fried okra on the house. Oh, and we don't get drunk in public; I won't have my employees sloppy drunk out places or getting arrested for being drunk."

"Fine by me."

"You aren't a drunkard, are you, Pax?"

"Not at all. I like a cold beer or two with a ballgame sometimes, but that's my limit."

"You're pretty easy going. Annie said you were. She's talked about this fine man she met on the Internet, the same site where people lie about themselves and one another and cheat and steal and bully. But now, Annie has said you checked out, and she did check you out 'cause she isn't a stupid woman, and she says you are one of the few, real good ones."

"She's one of the good ones."

"That she is," Coral agreed paternally, "one of the best. I won't abide her being hurt. That said, you seem okay to me, so I can give you a chance."

"I s'pect that means one chance only?"

"Yup."

"That's more than we get sometimes. Some folks...they don't use the chance given them."

"That's true."

Pax cocked his head. "Listen to that rain, wasn't a cloud in the sky when I came across the bridge, and now it's coming down hard, sounds like a bad spring storm." He enjoyed a good storm when he was in a house for the evening and not out somewhere.

"We get them bad at times. It does sound pretty rough out there, may slow business down some, but the spa patrons have to eat, and we're the best game in town."

Pax started to say something back, but they heard a loud crash of plates and cutlery and a squeal that was close to a full scream. Both men looked at one another in surprise, wondering if someone had been hurt. Coral ran to see what had happened because it was his diner; Pax went because Annie was out there and because he wanted to make sure she was all right.

He felt a tightness in his belly.

Pax suddenly understood why sometimes Katie whined and sniffed and just knew something felt wrong. Everything *sounded* wrong and *smelled* wrong. *It felt bad.* That's what Katie lived by.

Pax could almost smell the *wrongness* in the air.

Chapter 4

When they got to the dining area, both men stood still for a second, looking around because the scene simply didn't make sense to them. Everything had to be reconstructed. Bit by bit, they pieced it together. Lydia had dropped a pan of used plates, forks, spoons, and plastic glasses so that glass, bits of food, and gleaming ice cubes littered the floor in a mess. She stood still, her hands covering her mouth, maybe to keep herself from screaming fully as she stared at the doorway and side of the counter, wide eyed and scared. She was frozen in place.

That was where the main noise came from: the tray falling and her screaming. Coral and Pax had to go back farther in time to understand this, so they followed her gaze and took in everything.

The entire diner had gone silent; the only noises were the pounding rain and claps of thunder. It was a fairly strong storm that showed no signs of slowing. The windows were cloudy with fog and the driving rain, from outside. Each time the thunder rumbled, the rain drove in harder.

No one ate; everyone was letting his food go cold and instead, stared in the same direction as Lydia, face set in a mask of horror, confusion, and fear. No one moved other than to cast his eyes sideways to Coral.

A man in shorts and a tee-shirt sat on a stool at the far end of the counter near the door, his eyes lost and angry, a steak knife in one hand, blood covering both the blade and handle of the knife, as well as his hands and arms. He looked drenched with crimson, but he didn't brush it away.

Sweat poured down his face as his eyes rolled wildly. He was the kind of man that at best, people forgot or looked over, a nondescript man whose life's accomplishments might be a perfectly mowed lawn, never missing a day at a mundane job, and being a good usher at his smallish Methodist church. He was very ordinary except for the blood and the knife, and the fact that he seemed to care about neither.

Coral traded a quick glance with Pax and shifted his gaze.

At the man's feet beside the stool, lay a pretty little girl of about six or seven in a pool of blood that had poured from her chest; she might have been still breathing shallowly, but it was impossible to be sure. Her blue shorts and blue and pink tee shirt were bloodied; her blonde pigtails were crimson at the ends. Her little fingers were curled delicately.

The blood looked out of place, and had the girl not been at the center of it, it would have been surreal. It was so very red that it hardly seemed real.

Close to her was a toddler; his throat was cut and gaping open, and his little faded, denim bib overalls were a gory mess. He still had a pacifier in his mouth, and one hand gripped around a scruffy, stuffed blue rabbit. Blue eyes, wide and shocked, stared at the ceiling. One little foot stuck out; it was in a little Chuck Taylor sneaker, the laces undone and trailing into the blood; they were more red than white.

Coral found himself staring at the pacifier and the blue bunny. Nothing made sense. How had these children appeared on his floor, bleeding, and what did this mean? It related to the man who sat holding the knife, but Coral struggled to connect the dots.

A few feet away lay a pretty woman; she was curvaceous and wore a lime green halter with denim shorts and had hair that was long, dirty blonde and shiny, but she also lay in a pool of blood, her hands and arms bloodied from defensive wounds. Her chest was punctured several times. Her facial expression was one of shock and pain.

Another one. And this still made no sense.

Her umbrella lay to one side, still opened from when she had used it to keep the children and herself dry.

Bloody marks and water on the floor indicated someone had crawled or been dragged to a booth across from the man, and Coral and Pax hoped that whoever it was might still be alive. They couldn't see over the backs of the seats but knew the person needed first aid quickly. Coral was squeamish about blood, and all this red splashed everywhere made his stomach flip.

"What? What's going on?" Coral asked Dana, the other waitress. He was still trying to reason this out.

"He...he...Oh, my God, Coral, they came in, and he...he was yelling...Yelling like loud hissing...mad but not loud. He picked up a knife off the counter that someone had left: the man who had a steak and that baked potato with chili; this man just...just...did that. He grabbed the knife and did it. To his family, he did that right here." Her hands were at her chin and mouth, white with tension.

She stared accusingly at the man at the counter.

Seeing her white skin and the way she shook, Coral whispered for her to sit down before she passed out. She slid to the floor, weeping. Okay, he had information. He got it. It was bizarre, but he made more sense of the scene now.

Coral made motions with his hands to the patrons watching him that they should be quiet, be calm, and stay seated at their tables or in their booths. Everyone was still terrified but also felt safer with the big man there and in charge of the situation.

He called out, "Hello, there. I'm Coral, and this is my place. How can I help you?" in a friendly, calm way, he asked the man with the knife. He felt fainty insane, trying to speak calmly with a man who had by all accounts, just slaughtered at least three people.

The man mumbled. At least he was responsive, so Coral could possibly get a feel for what was going on in the man's head. "Pardon? I didn't get that."

Another mumble.

"What's your name?"

"Ed. I'm Ed," the man moaned, rubbing at his wet hair and head. He was soaked with rain.

"Well, Ed, what can I do for you?"

"Worms."

Coral cocked his head. "Worms, Ed? You want some worms?"

"They're here."

"Where are they? Are they in here? I sure don't care for worms unless I'm baiting a hook and fishin'."

"In my head."

"The worms are in your head?"

Ed mumbled a yes.

"Oh. That's terrible. We need to get you some help quickly." Coral noted that none of the diners happened to be the local policemen tonight; they usually dropped in a little later. It figured when he needed them, they wouldn't be here. "We can get those worms out and make you feel a little better. We'll get you help"

"I don't want help. It's getting better. It's all getting better," said the man who had lost the anger in his eyes and looked almost peaceful.

"Okay, well, what is it you do want?"

Pax admired the man's calm voice and control as he reached slowly towards Annie. Moving by inches, she crept closer to him, leaned into him, and grabbed for his hand; he sighed. Just holding her hand and knowing she was safe and he was between the crazy guy and her, made him feel better.

"I don't want anything. I want the worms to stop whispering. They'll be finished soon though."

"I would think so." Coral took a step closer to the man, his hands in plain sight, making him look smaller as he moved. "How did they get into your head?"

"I dunno. Damned things." The man cast red, angry eyes at Coral. "They're pissing me off, taking too long."

"Were they in your family, too?"

"How would I know? I don't know shit about the things. My head hurts." He casually slid the blade across his palm; Coral and Pax could see he had done this before as three deep, bloody cuts were already there. "Ahhh."

"The rest here don't have them, and we don't want them to get worms either; what say we let them all leave? And then we can figure out what to do to get the ones in your head out? We don't need pesky whispering worms."

"No."

"No?"

"I said no. I may not be finished."

"I see."

"They should do it, too. It's peaceful other than their itching."

"Okay." Coral slid a few steps closer. I may not be finished, the man had just said. He heard odd sounds from the booth where the blood trail led; there was a sound like duct tape being ripped and some cracks and pops. It made him think someone had survived. Without help, the person could be bleeding out, but Coral thought the man, Ed, might attack him if he made a sudden move.

A loud cacophony of thunder exploded overhead, making everyone jump.

Coral used the distraction to slide another foot closer.

Pax squeezed Annie's hand. If everything else felt surreal, at least she felt real and stable.

"I feel free," Ed said suddenly, "except for the worms. They itch."

"Well, that must feel good to be free. I sure would appreciate it if you'd allow me to clean up this mess. I just hate a messy diner."

"Mess?" The man looked about at his slaughtered family with little concern.

Coral nodded. "So no one slips on the wet floor."

"If you must. Ducks. But I may not be red finished...." Ed rolled the knife's handle in his fingers so it glittered dangerously; the threat was clear. "Pretty soon, I won't care. I will even eat my wife's meatloaf." He chuckled, staring at her body. "Except she's dead, huh?"

"I don't know if she is. I can check. Also, I can send my staff for a mop bucket and mop...."

Coral was wondering what to do as he mulled over what this had to do with ducks or meatloaf.

"No," Ed said, "she bitched a lot. The kids were loud a lot. The worms are spaghetti in my cake." He rubbed his head again.Coral suppressed a frown of confusion. "It's over now, no more bitchin' or loudness, right? No more spaghetti in your cake." For one second, Coral was afraid he would laugh at the crazy words. He knew if he did laugh, he would just laugh and laugh until he went mad because it wasn't a funny, silly chuckle trying to escape him.

It was a scared noise that wanted out. Oh yes, when the spaghetti was in your cake, then it was a time to laugh until tears ran down your cheeks because otherwise, you would sit down and scream a good, long time. If Coral didn't keep his thoughts in one tiny spot in his brain, he would start looking at the tiny sneaker in the blood and that little girl with her pink-tipped hair, and they would wonder why he or someone else hadn't saved them, and well, that was when all would just go to hell.

He took another step, biting on his cheek with his teeth to keep focused. From the side, he could see into the booth now, but what he saw made less sense than Ed's rambling. Maybe it was because he was straining his eyes sideways to try to see what was there.

Another step didn't help sort what he was seeing.

A boy, maybe a pre-teen, was lying on his stomach with his face and head turned to one side. He was partially under the table, tangled around the pedestal, and sticky crimson was all over the floor.

A man sat on the boy's back with one of the diner's knives; the man was carefully worrying at the flesh on the boy's neck and upper back and arms. He had torn the tee shirt down the middle to expose the boy's back.

Now, the man was cutting and snapping the small bones in one of the boy's hands but then dropped the hand and went back to the back. To Coral's horror, the man ripped off a section of skin with a duct-tape kind of sound and popped it into his mouth like a treat, chewing complacently.

He had already eaten a good deal of the flesh.

Coral gagged. A giggle rose. The spaghetti was in the cake. Watching Coral, Pax and the others wondered what had made the big man sick enough to gag and to turn pale. Coral's face twitched as if he were trying not to laugh, and Pax saw the beginnings of acute shock taking over his new friend.

"Rock steady, Coral," Pax called out.

Pax felt Annie moving slowly, and something was pushed into Pax's hand. It was the handle of a steak knife. He longed to feel the handle of a revolver instead, but this was better than nothing, maybe.

"I have one, too," she whispered. Pax admired her bravery and fortitude right then; she was calm and thinking hard. No matter what, she was setting up a second line of protection for these people and willing to fight. Even across the Internet in chats, Pax had felt she was a survivor and a strong, good person who would step up if needed.

What if Pax hadn't come to Cold Springs? What if Annie were here facing this without him? He shivered, thinking he would have been horrified for her.

Ed jerked his head toward them, and a frightening second passed while Pax wondered if he were about to be in a knife fight. Ed was only casually watching Coral who was still pale but was actively trying to concentrate on Ed again. Everyone watching was trying to guess what had so unnerved the big football player.

"He was hungry," Ed said to Coral with a head nod to the action in the booth. "Very hungry."

Pax felt a stone lodge in his belly. Ed's comments sounded as if...well, Pax could hardly comprehend the rest of his thought. He tilted his head a little. What could make someone do something so terrible to another?

Coral barely nodded back, confirming Pax's worst scenario; Pax swallowed hard.

"I see that," Coral said conversationally. He watched the man chewing on the boy and then almost fell over in shock as the man turned around so that Coral could see his face. Despite his face and chest and hands being red with slippery blood and his clothes being rain soaked, the man was someone Coral had known well; for years, he had known Myke who ran the antique shop right down the street and was one of the sanest, nicest fellows anyone would ever want to meet; he wasn't violent, and he certainly wasn't a cannibal. {Not that he knew what a cannibal looked like particularly}.

"Hi, Myke," Coral said, unsure what he should say.

Myke groaned and muttered something, suddenly seeming to be more aware of what he was doing, wiped his mouth with a sleeve and crawled off the boy to lean against the seats, his feet in the aisle. His eyes were calm, uncaring, and mild as he yawned. "Hmmm," he said to Coral.

As the rest of the people in the diner saw who it was, they gasped; when they saw his bloodied mouth and teeth, they moaned and whined, wondering if Myke had been under the table doing something very horrible.

Coral wanted to keep Ed in his sights, but he couldn't look away from the gore of the boy's neck and back and Myke's eyes, which were like watching a flame burning, but a flame that was getting smaller and duller by the second. Beside his leg, Coral twitched his fingers, willing Pax to be ready to help him and be able to.

Pax moved away from Annie, motioning her to stay put, as he hid the knife behind his back and took a few sliding steps towards Coral and the carnage at the door. He tried to keep his body loose and ready for anything. His movements would let Coral know he was going to try to help. Despite her moxie, Annie wasn't the type for a knife fight, and neither was anyone else; this was all on Pax. He was watching Ed's gaze going dimmer. "Hi, Ed. I'm Pax."

"Paz? Paz, I have bugles in my frog. Tired."

Coral glanced back to Ed. "That's a shame. Let's relax, buddy. Put down the knife, and we'll talk some more; knives make me nervous."

Ed looked at the blade as if he didn't know why he was holding it. He spoke calmly and seemed passive now. "I don't know, maybe."

Coral moved like the lightning that flashed outside the diner, feinting right and then darting in from the left, plowing into Ed and the stool, heaving all his weight at the man holding the knife. Both men went sprawling in a huge explosive noise that made everyone cringe and jump with fear. Someone screamed. It was a classic tackle, and the knife fumbled into the air where it twirled a long second and fell to the ground.

Myke didn't even blink as Pax rushed him. Pax kicked the knife away so that it skittered across the floor, spinning, as he yanked the man to his feet, swinging him around and snapping the man's arm into a tight arm lock that would have made most men howl. Myke didn't utter a word but just stared calmly at the diners. Pax knew the hold must hurt, but he was scared and nervous about this.

A woman in a booth recoiled from Myke's dirty, red-stained teeth.

In a second, Coral had Ed in the same position. "Get some table cloths, and rip 'em into strips so we can use them as rope, hurry."

Annie, Lydia, Dana, and a few others sprang into action, ripping and making strips of the cloth, yanking and jerking each strip to test the knots. While neither man tried to get away, it was if everyone expected both to try soon.

"Bugles out of the frogs now, Ed? Worms out of the cake?" Pax shook as he snapped the words. "What a mess. What in the hell are we going to do with all this mess?"

Chapter 5

Both Pax and Coral, using the strips of cloth as makeshift ropes, securely tied the men's hands behind their backs. After tossing the men into booths, Pax tied their ankles as well. Neither captive reacted but lay in the booth seats complacently, their eyes dead. "Ed? Hey, Ed? Myke?" Coral tried, but he got no reaction.

"What happened? Give me the story?" Coral asked. He sat for a second on a stool and drank strong tea that Annie slid to him, swallowing half of the glassful as fast as he could. His mouth was like cotton.

Everything had happened so fast, and the situation wasn't good, but Pax couldn't help but replay in his mind what Coral had done. The man may have retired from playing professional football, but he had lost none of his power and grace. When Coral tackled Ed, the tackle was perfectly executed, and for those seconds, Coral had been fully in charge.

Dana shivered. "Ed came in dripping wet, and his family was behind him with the umbrella, okay? They were huddled under it to keep dry. I could tell he must have been complaining or yelling at them; they looked upset and nervous, his family I mean. Not bad upset, just uncomfortable you know as if they were tired and needed something to eat and drink."

Coral nodded. A lot of time, tourists had little problems as they went from the spa to shops to shops; mostly, they needed to either warm up or cool down and to hydrate. It was fairly amazing how many people felt poorly simply because they failed to stay hydrated. Once they had some water in them, Coral's good cooking did the rest: gave them energy, comforted the body and senses, and afforded them a chance to feel better. A short time off their feet, and a bathroom break did the rest.

Dana continued, "He shook off like a dog, and I could see he was really pissed off. I dreaded serving him 'cause he was gonna be a complainer, but maybe he was just being hungry. So I was about to offer to seat them, but then he just looked right at the knife sitting on the counter, grabbed it off the plate, and stabbed the little girl. He didn't say a word first, just shoved it into her chest as if the action was the most natural thing on earth."

"He didn't say anything?" Pax asked.

"Not a thing."

From a booth, a man named Dan, nodded. "I saw it, but it was as if I was seeing a nightmare, not real. I thought I had to be hallucinating 'cause Dana's right, he didn't say a thing, just glared angrily, and the little girl...her mouth opened in a big O-shape like she couldn't believe it either."

Dana rubbed her arms as if she were cold. "I thought I was the only one watching it particularly...and I thought...well, like Dan said...it wasn't real. It couldn't be real, and I saw it, but I just froze."

"My, God," Coral said, half in prayer.

"It was really fast...a blink, and it was over, but it was also very slow. I could see a raindrop fall from the man's nose and onto the little girl's shirt. That damned drop fell for...it seemed like weeks...so slowly...."

"I couldn't move, Boss, even if I wanted to stop him or run away. I was frozen to the spot. All around me, I could hear people eating, silverware clinking, and everyone talking, but I was frozen and felt as if I were the only one watching him."

"You were in shock, I guess," Coral said. "I guess you both were." He looked to Pax. "No one expected to see that, and sometimes people freeze with fear.

The body chemicals do something, I guess." Pax didn't know, but it made sense that it could be true. He wanted to agree with Coral anyway and keep them all calm.

"Maybe so. He killed the teen kid who was just staring and making this *guh guh guh* sound, and then next was the little boy. It was like Dan said, very fast, so fast I could hardly see it all, but it was also very, horribly slow, too, and his wife yanked at him and screamed."

"She let loose a big scream," Dan agreed, "That's when everyone noticed."

Dana sniffled and wiped her nose with her arm. "They stopped eating and talking. I didn't feel so alone then. Lydia dropped the tray she was carrying; Coral, it was as if time started acting normal again."

Lydia nodded her head. "I couldn't take it all in."

Dan made a motion with his hand, as if he were stabbing with an imaginary knife across the air. "He stabbed at her...at his wife, and then she fell, and you ran in, Coral. I don't think anyone could have done a thing; it was a bad thing for sure."

"Happened really fast?"

"Super fast, but I couldn't say a word or do anything. I froze, and blood was all over, and when Lydia dropped the tray, everyone turned around and saw the whole thing. You'd think people would have been screaming, but the situation was as if it were not real...." Dana was repeating herself. "I wish...."

"What happened with Myke? How did he get into this mess?"

Dana looked at Myke, trussed up and lying in the booth. "Myke came in almost at the same time, a half minute behind, I guess, when that Ed guy was stabbing his wife, and he...Myke, I mean...grabbed the kid and dragged him over there and...." she gagged. "They didn't say anything. It happened really fast, Coral."

Pax was a little confused. "You *know* that guy?"

"Sure we do," Coral answered.

Dan squinted a little. "When I saw it, I thought that Myke was here to help and wasn't that a *splendid* turn of events to have him rush in and pull the boy to safety. It was as if everything were going to be fine because we had help. I wanted to jump up and help, too. I was *going* to, but then you came in, Coral, and that guy said all that stuff; I just don't know."

"We didn't move. He might have come after us," a man added.

"Yup. He had a wicked look on his face; he would've," Dan added again. There should be more to talk about, and police would have questions, but the topic was fizzling. With Ed not talking anymore and the action being over, and its having ended on a bad note, there wasn't much else to say. No one could think of what to add unless he repeated it all.

"Coral, oh, hells bells, lookit that," a man yelled.

Chapter 6

"Oh, my God," a woman yelled, "Look out there." She was pointing to the big picture window where she sat.

One end of Coral's Diner faced Hickory where the parking lot was; the door was at that end. The long side of the place faced 2nd Street, across from the farmer's market and the park. The other end faced Main, the Catholic Church, and Clothes Horse, a clothing store.

All turned to look out the window where they watched two men beating on each other but with a certain lack of enthusiasm; their fight brought them alongside the diner's window. Both men had hit one another enough that both had bruised faces, swollen noses that bled, and squinting, blackened eyes.

Yet they were either tired *of* the fight, tired *from* the fight, or just *bored*. Both the original fury and interest were gone.

It may have looked like a normal brawl where possibly one man was drunk, or they were fighting over a female; however, the intensity and then focus that each man had towards the fight were unmistakable.

In a last burst of energy, one of the men surged forward at the other, gouging at the other man's eyes with his nails as they fought under the lights.

The second man collapsed under the new assault, sinking onto the wet ground, howling and throwing his arms to his sides in a gesture that made it seem as if he were giving up.

The bigger man crawled onto the other man's chest to hold him down on the wet ground; both of his thumbnails sank into the man's sockets, popping the eyeballs loose as he worried and worked at them. It wasn't easily done; in fact, it took a lot of hard work and determination.

The attack was less an assault than a behavior that was inflicted with a definite need, passion for the job, and anger at the other person. It wasn't a random act but a duty to do this to one another.

Someone in the diner screamed, and another yelped as they watched. It seemed less real than something that might be on the television.

"What is going on?" someone demanded.

Coral didn't have an answer. Besides hating to see the violence, Coral was curious and wondered why the men were fighting to the death, but you couldn't have paid him to go out there in the falling rain. Like everyone else, he knew something was terribly wrong.

The man with torn-out eyes reached blindly for his adversary, but the other man seemed to have lost interest and stood in the rain as if he were showering, rubbing the water into his skin, and letting the rain clean the blood from his hands.

In a few seconds, he turned and walked away into the gathering dusk as if nothing had occurred, taking his time, but not looking around as he walked down the street.

The man on the ground turned his head to the side, away from the onlookers, and didn't move any more.

Over kitty-corner to Coral's Diner at the Clothes Horse, a trendy clothing shop, a car drove into the front windows, reversed, and drove back again into the rubble. The movements were slow and methodical.

Among the clothes, a mashed mess on the hood, and spider-webbed windshield was probably a body but was too banged up for anyone to be sure.

A second figure, waving arms and crying out, was mashed into the bricks and glass; each time the car reversed, the figure weakly waved an arm, and when the car surged forward, the figure tensed as it was shoved

"We need to do something," Dan suggested, but no one responded.

He might have repeated his statement, but something new occurred.

Chapter 7

Two people walked up, and one opened the door to the diner. Everyone stared at them, jumping as the door opened. Coral wished he had locked the door, but it was too late. He felt a horrible dread in his gut.

One was Marla, a woman they knew, an exuberant, almost hyper-active woman who was always full of energy and excitable, but today, she moved slowly, shaking off rain onto the floor and rubbing at her arms.

Brushing at the rain did nothing to dry her because she was completely soaked to the skin. She looked around at the blood and carnage with little interest, not really paying attention to it as she stepped over the blood.

Stepping around the bodies, she walked over to the counter just as she had many times before. Rain dripped from her hair.

The person with her was Gus from the gasoline station, and he stripped off a slicker and tossed an umbrella to one side. Gus promptly took in the scene, groaned, and nearly vomited on the floor, gagging instead. Looking away from the gore, he half-waved, "Sorry, Coral, but jeez...here, too?"

"Too? What do you mean?"

"I mean it's crazy all over town. Didn't you know?"

"We just found out it was crazy in *here*," Coral said as he looked around to include everyone watching the exchange.

"Sorry, I almost barfed on your floor, Coral, but it's a mess anyway...umm...it's not just here."

"And out there...I mean we saw out the window...some stuff...people beating on each other and a car running back and forth to The Clothes Horse." Coral was almost worried about being believed.

"This?" Gus gestured around the diner. "This is what's out there. I saw that car; it's Marybeth Hanover in the car, and she ran over...well...not sure who it is on her windshield, but he's dead whoever it is. *I hope*. And she is smashing someone right into the bricks, enough to make you sick. I did get sick out there walking over."

"Marybeth? Ain't no way," someone yelled.

"Are you sure, Gus? Marybeth is a good person and not likely to do that." Coral said, but then, Myke was a good person, too. His head was dizzy from trying to make sense of all the craziness. Pax, new to town, must think that all of the townspeople are insane to go around killing each other with knives and cars.

What did it matter how low their crime rate? In one night, they had a killer with a knife butcher his family in front of an audience, a man turn cannibal, and a murderer using her car to plow through people?

Gus went on with his news, "On the way over, I saw Rick in his patrol car, mowing down anyone on the street just…running them down, Rick! Can you imagine that?"

Someone called out, "What have you been drinking, Gus?"

"Nothing. I'm sober as can be."

"He's drunk, Coral."

Coral knew Gus wasn't drunk. Unfortunately, everything Gus said was probably true.

"You didn't see Rick doing that," the heckler called out.

"I saw him, too. He was wet-haired, but he was driving the patrol car, and he got three or four that I saw."

Everyone snapped heads to look at Coral.

Coral shook his head, trying to imagine the dedicated, pleasant police officer, Rick, using his patrol car as a weapon for murder.

It defied imagination, but Gus wasn't one to drink or imagine things or to lie. "Let's let Gus finish and hear him out. He ain't one to go around lying, especially at a time like this. Let him talk."

"Seems fair," Pax agreed.

"That isn't like Rick," Coral told Pax.

Gus went on, still kind of green as he walked past the mess on the floor, glanced at the tied men, curiously, and leaned against the snack bar."

Then I saw two people I don't know fighting…tourists, maybe…one was beating the head of the other into the concrete.

Some others were just walking in the rain as if they were out for a stroll, looking at the fight going on and not even caring. What the hell is going on?"

"Rick is about the most normal, sane person I know," someone said.

"Well, he isn't right now," Gus said, "has everyone gone crazy?"

"We don't know. We had this happen and saw the trouble outside; now, you are saying that it's all over. I don't know what to think," Coral admitted. "But I guess we can put our heads together and figure it out."

"We'll have to," Pax agreed.

"I was walking up and saw Marla, so we walked the rest of the way across the street together. I have been trying to find some sane people, not attacking each other. But like I said, 'I saw Marybeth with that body on the car and got sick, but Marla, she didn't even react,' " Gus said.

Coral looked at the woman curiously, wondering what was wrong with her.

Marla looked at the bodies casually, surveyed the diner, and sat down on a stool with her face a total blank.

Coral looked her over. "Hi, Marla."

She barely lifted a hand in greeting. "Meat loaf," she said dully.

"You want meatloaf?" Coral asked, concerned with her tone and body language. "Are you injured, Marla?" Had she seen something to make her behave this way? Was she okay or not?

"Everything is fine," she said.

"Shock?" Pax asked, " maybe we need to do something for her...."

Coral looked her over, stared into Marla's eyes, and felt her hands which were warm and not ice cold as they would have been had she been in shock. "No shock I ever saw. She acts...empty...just empty." Coral shook his head as he stepped back to speak to Pax quietly. "Marla is a screamer and hyper; this is not like her. It doesn't look like shock to me."

For some reason, Coral thought about the *spaghetti in the*

cake and *the bugles in the frog* that Ed had talked about and had a sinking feeling that Marla, a woman he had known for years, might clearly understand that gibberish.

"Is she okay?"

The woman was wearing a white blouse with blue jeans, but the shirt had gone pink with rain-soaked blood. "It's isn't her blood." He raised Marla's arms, and she held them there. She was like a giant doll he could pose. Although he asked her questions and spoke to her, she didn't say anything clear, only mumbled a few times.

"She's like Ed and Myke after they had finished," Pax said quietly.

"Why are they like zombies?" Dana asked. "That guy, Ed, was all angry; now he's like a zombie, no reactions, Myke, too. They don't care that they're tied up. And Marla, look at her. Why are they acting as if they're empty?"

Had she been upset when she had asked that question, Coral would have ushered her to the back before she started a panic, but Dana was calm. People nodded with every question she asked. It was what they were all wondering.

They turned to the window as Coral stared at the action outside; the car had finally stopped pushing into the building and was stopped in the parking lot. Coral realized it *was* Marybeth's car, and as he heard gasps from other people, he knew they had noticed the same thing.

The bundle of rags, *the body,* was still lodged into the windshield, but at least the car had stopped. All sighed as if they had been holding a collective breath. The blinded man still lay on the grass, letting the rain continue to fall into his face, but he didn't seem to be in pain or upset. No one could tell if he were breathing or not.

It was finally hitting all of them.

"People are violent, I mean, to the ultimate; then, they just get blank looking and go away, so they're like zombies," Dana said.

"No such thing, Dana. Zombies are make-believe."

"Must be a poison gas," someone suggested, "they're sick."

"Them damned North Koreans."

"We'd all be affected" Coral disagreed. He didn't think North Korea had bombed Cold Springs with poison gas. "It isn't gas. You ever heard of a gas picking people out?" Despite himself, he looked back at the toddler's little sneaker. *Spaghetti in the cake.* "It's something else."

"A virus?"

"I don't know. It doesn't feel like it is," Pax said. He didn't know what a virus that made people react so violently would feel like, but people weren't acting in ways that would indicate an illness. He didn't know what to think.

"Something in the water?"

"Coral's cooking?" A few chuckled, easing the tension.

"Hey," Coral grumbled.

"Why would it be affecting a few like that? You ever heard of a virus that does that? Not unless it's a zombie virus, like Dana said; they're becoming zombies and attacking," a woman said.

"I didn't say all that," Dana argued.

"Myke was chewing on that kid like a zombie." The buzz was getting louder as people began to agree. The crowd had gone from ignoring the slashing of a family and freezing in place as they watched to building a theory of a zombie virus going around.

Coral rubbed the back of his head and hoped his headache would hold off. He raised his voice, "No one is a zombie. There is no zombie virus. If there were, we'd see a bunch of people munching on others by now, ok? There are no zombies. Zombies don't drive cars. Period. Try to be helpful, or don't say anything, okay?"

"Zombies don't drive cars? That's the best you have?" Pax almost chuckled.

Coral snickered. Dana started giggling. It was inappropriate, maybe, but several started laughing.

Coral shrugged, "Hey, it's the best I could think of. Have you ever seen a zombie behind the wheel?"

More laughs followed.

Chapter 8

"They're all wet," Annie said. She pointed to the men outside and at Marla and Ed and then Myke.

"So?" a woman asked.

"So the ones who are violent are wet, and then they go blank and empty after they act out."

Dana shook her head. "Gus was out there in the rain, too. He isn't violent or empty."

"He was in a slicker and had an umbrella," Annie said. "Did you get wet, Gus?" Her eyes glittered as she spoke, her brain working furiously. Coral had always teased her that when she was really thinking, it showed on her face.

"Dry as can be," Gus said. He went around the counter and poured himself steaming coffee and brought out the carafe to share with others, making himself at home. "But people out there, they are wet for sure. They're out there beating on each other and doing things in the rain." He nodded, beginning to understand Annie's train of thought.

"But rain? Really?" Coral asked, "how? why?"

"I don't know, but the violent ones are rain soaked. Now, they aren't violent but just *smoothed out.*"

"Smooth?" Pax cocked his head as he thought that over.

Annie looked at Marla and then again at Pax. "Smooth, nothing there. In rivers, water...it smoothes out rocks. That's what I was thinking."

Pax frowned. "It's about as possible as a zombie virus, right? Maybe something is in the rain, a pollutant."

A man and woman watching out the window nervously stood together, sharing glances. He was tall and had a bit of a potbelly that stretched his thin tee shirt; she was small and flat across the chest, dressed in oft-washed shorts and a tee shirt. The man threw cash and change on the table beside their half-finished, cold dinners. They spoke in low tones, still looking out the window.

Everyone in the diner looked at the man and woman as they stood. It was clear what they intended to do.

Annie spoke up and addressed the couple that were standing and holding hands; they were heading for the door. "Hey, don't go out there. I may be totally wrong here, but what if what I said is right?"

"That's what I said...." the woman began, but a sharp glance from her husband silenced her.

They were scared, that much was clear, and the fear showed in their eyes, but they also had the look of creatures that were ready to turn and run full out. They looked as afraid of the people in the diner as any outside the building.

"This is ridiculous, and we are getting out of here and out of this freaking town." The man pulled at his wife's hand. "You folks deal with it. We don't want any part of this; I'm sorry it's a mess and that this is happening, but we're leaving. You have a problem here. But, this isn't our problem. We're going to leave and go to the next town; you can handle things here."

The woman shrugged and sighed with a little nod.

"You'll get soaked," Annie said. *She wanted to tell them they were damned idiots and they were going to get killed out there.*

The man looked at the umbrella the woman and children had used, but it was sitting in a pool of blood. "We'll run for it, and the car is just around the side of the building; we'd rather get soaked than stay in this place," the man told his wife.

"You won't like it out there, especially if Rick runs into you with his patrol car," Gus said.

"You saw that car; it ran over someone, and you saw those two men and what happened in here, and you heard Gus. It isn't safe out there, regardless of what the cause is," Coral added. He felt responsible since they were safe in *his* diner, but he couldn't force them to stay.

The man narrowed his eyes and said, "We're going to run." He looked to his wife, "If anyone tries anything, keep running...."

"Are you sure?" Coral wondered if the man were pressuring his wife and asked her the question.

She nodded.

"Don't start; we're out of here. This just isn't our problem. It's your town, not ours," the man said, "sorry, I hope it works out for you."

They ran out, tracking blood across to the door as they stepped in it, grimacing as their tennis shoes made sticky sounds. The crime scene was being ruined. Annie ran over to press her face to the glass, watching the couple. Others watched as well, dreading what might happen but also seeing it as an experiment for their theory.

Outside, the man and woman splashed in puddles, darting over to dryer areas, batting at the water. Then, they stopped for a second under the sheets of hard rain, looking up, as if they had just really noticed the rain and liked it. They paused, kind of rubbing the water into their skin in a strange way. They didn't run anymore but stood in the downpour, letting it sluice over their bodies, soaking them.

"Damn," asked Coral as he breathed hard, "why are they doing that?" For some reason, the thought of rubbing the water into his skin made him feel squirmy. His heart hammered.

"Why aren't they running?" someone else asked.

"It wasn't the plan to stop like that," Annie muttered, "I think it's the rain."

Outside, the woman yanked at her shirt, tearing it down the middle, exposing her white bra and small breasts. All at once, she lunged for her husband's neck, clawing at his skin with her long, red nails, and although no one could hear her, she was snarling and hissing like a wild animal, her pretty face wild and aggressive.

Her husband backhanded her hard, knocking her down into the soaked grass and mud; she was up like a cat, scratching at his throat again. He yanked for his car keys, threaded on a big fob in his pocket, and began to stab her face and arms, drawing blood. She recoiled from the stabs but stayed close to him, scratching.

"Oh, my God," Annie whispered. People who were watching, muttered and gasped.

"Is it the water?" Lydia asked as she rubbed the window, wiping away the fog from her breath so that she could see more clearly.

"We have to do something," a man said, but no one moved.

In a few seconds, the woman, outside, grabbed a broken

stick from the ground and began to poke at her husband's neck until he was bleeding, too. He dodged her, but she used it as a fencing sword, poking and jabbing. The damage to his neck wasn't huge, just cuts and stabs, but the man was furious.

Dropping his keys in the mud, the man ran across the street to the car that had been bashing into the clothing store, side stepped it, snagged a sliver of glass from the front window of the shop, and ran back at his wife, brandishing it like a knife.

"Oh, no," Annie moaned. People had gathered close to her to stare out the windows and were relaying what was happening to the rest. in the diner.

The woman tried to out maneuver him, but he slashed at her violently, slicing his own palms open as he did so. He cut his wife's face, slicing into one cheek and ruining her looks.

As his brain itched, he stabbed again and again, poking at her chest, throat, and face; her hands were sliced and stabbed as she tried to defend herself, the broken stick was tossed away as the battle escalated.

The man made one more lunge at her, skewering her in the throat, and then, as she reeled backwards, he lost interest in her and dropped the shard of glass to the ground. Falling, his wife curled up on the wet grass, bleeding to death from several wounds, her throat pouring blood that washed away into the soil, twitching with residual pain and fury that were draining out of her with the water.

Her thoughts were washed away.

As everyone watched, the man dropped his arms as if the energy had left him and he had burned out; he walked away through the pouring rain with his hands cut from wielding the shard of glass. He didn't look back at the diner or pick up his car keys.

"It's the rain," Annie said.

"Not necessarily," Coral said as he seemed less sure now. He shook his head as he watched the fight outside. Had he been positive it wasn't the rain, wouldn't he have run out there to help the woman? Wouldn't Pax have? Wouldn't others have bolted to her aid? But they didn't because they were thinking the same thing. He wasn't ready to agree it was the rain, but he wasn't able to debate it either, now that he had seen the fight outside.

Pax looked horrified at what had happened in the rain.

Chapter 9

"They were fine, and then the people saw them go into the rain and almost bathe in it; then, do that...that wasn't normal. It has to be the rain," Annie said.

"What kind of rain would do that?" Lydia asked.

"I don't know. I bet Marla was violent before she went all smooth."

Marla didn't react to Annie's accusations.

Annie looked at the pink stains on Marla's shirt. "Did you hurt someone, Marla?"

Lydia came back into the main area. "Police said they'd get over here in a while since we have it under *control* and it's not an *emergency*; they said to stay *inside* and to lock the doors, Coral."

"This isn't an emergency?" Pax asked.

Lydia shook her head. "They have a lot of problems going on all over town, and right when we were talking, the phone went dead, and it's not working, now," Lydia reported. "And Dana and I can't get cell phone bars, either."

"This is going on all over town!" Coral roared.

"I said it was," Gus said quietly.

Coral just stared at Gus; yes, he had told them, but it was a little different hearing it from the police. And, that made Coral think again about the fact that Gus had said one of the police officers was one of the ones running over people with a patrol car.

"Don't hate the messenger; that's what they said. They have problems all over town with everyone's assaulting everyone else. They said to stay where we are and stay out of the rain," Lydia told him.

"That's pretty crazy," Gus said, "but I saw it myself. I told all of you."

"I said it was the rain," Annie said, moving away from the window and glaring at those who watched her. "Didn't I say it?"

Coral went to lock all the doors. "Okay. Fine. You said it. I can accept it."

Pax asked if Lydia, Dana, and Annie could get people tea or coffee and keep them calm. He asked a couple of men who volunteered to help cover the bodies with tablecloths. 'Crime scene be damned,' he thought.

Leaning on the counter, Pax looked at Marla carefully. "Marla? Hello, I'm Pax, Annie's friend. How are you?"

"I'm fine, Pax."

"I see you have some blood stains. They don't seem to be yours; did something happen out there?"

"I don't remember anything happening." She didn't seem curious.

"We had an incident here. I'm sure seeing that as you came in was a shock," Pax said, watching her eyes.

With as neutral tone, Marla responded, "It's okay, Pax. Things happen."

"Pretty scary evening, huh?"

"Is it?" She didn't seem afraid in the least.

"Do you have family you're worried about?"

She looked as if she had to think about that and then shrugged, "Everything is fine, isn't it? I'm sure there are no problems."

Annie paused. "Who is with Kerry?" She leaned towards Pax. "Kerry is five."

"I guess the babysitter. There's nothing to be concerned about."

"Marla, I have known you for years, and normally, you'd be bouncing off the walls, upset over the violence that happened here, and you'd be going crazy bitchin' about getting home to Kerry or at least pissed off about the phones and not being able to call Kerry."

"Everything is fine, Annie."

"What if someone has hurt or killed your child?" Pax hissed.

Annie's eyes went wide at what he said, wondering how he could be so hateful, but Marla's calm expression didn't change. No emotion was on her face or in her eyes. Annie understood now that Pax was doing a little experiment.

"It's all fine," Marla repeated.

"Okay. Just sit right here, and if those crazies break in, try not to get murdered," Pax whispered in one more attempt to get a reaction. Marla nodded, sitting like a manikin.

He thought about reaching out a finger to touch her wet shirt, to get some rain on him, just a drop on a single digit, to see if it felt different or anything happened, but he couldn't do it.

He was afraid. He knew that. He wasn't the type to be afraid; he was a concrete thinker, usually, happy to do hard labor as a contractor, building houses, not thinking, but soaking up the sun, and doing an excellent job for fair pay. He wasn't prone to imaginative thoughts or fears. He didn't worry about the dark, spiders, or the boogieman, but the truth was, he was scared as hell right now.

"Okay, Pax," Marla said.

He pulled Annie to the side. "That was weird. Annie; this is bad, really bad."

"It's weirder if you knew her before. She is the one who would be hysterical and loud, very emotional. This is not normal for her," Annie pointed out, "that isn't the Myke I know, either."

Coral got everyone's attention. "Look, none of us know what's happening. We've seen way too much violence and some major personality shifts, and all we know is that every one affected has been out in the rain.

The good news is that we have plenty of food here and that we're dry. The police know what's going on and will be here in a while. I am gonna go in the back and cook for all of you; your dinners are cold, and you know food soothes all problems. So you tell the ladies what you want, and it's on the house. If you have eaten already, enjoy some dessert and coffee on me, okay? Whatever you want, you can have."

The waitresses forced themselves to smile a little and take new orders and clean off tables, and the diners began to speak again, but it was quieter, now.

Coral asked Pax to watch the front as a kind of security and pointed out a few people he thought would help Pax keep the diner safe, or at least give the illusion of safety; safety was always an illusion.

For a second, Pax was surprised that Coral was entrusting him, especially since Pax was scared shitless, but the trust calmed him a little.

Pax found that his first job consisted of calming Lydia when she had a short, small break down and wept over the dropped and broken dishes. The events of the evening had finally hit her. She scooped up dishes while cutting her eyes over to look at the dead family. Now that there was a lull, she was about to fall apart. Pax told her to get orders while he threw the dishes into the grey pan.

Annie mouthed *thank you* to Pax as he patted Lydia and reassured her.

Pax didn't have time to be subtle. "George, Dan, Jake, and Jobie, he recited the names Coral had given him, can you help me with clean up and with making this place safe by keeping a look out?" When he called out the names, he wondered who each was. As they stood in response, he gave them nods. "Coral said I could depend on all of you."

George was an older man, and he nodded as he got up, patted his wife's hand and walked over to Pax to shake his hand. George was a former firefighter who had lived in Cold Springs all of his life, and Coral had whispered that the man was loyal, brave, and strong, despite his age. He also had experience with first aid and rescue. "We'll get things organized and make sure everyone feels safe here."

Dan was a farmer that Coral liked because he was a smart fellow and a quick thinker; he had already spoken up; people listened to him when they needed to hear common sense. He grabbed a broom and helped Lydia get the floor cleared, reassuring her everything was going to be okay. Dan chattered as he worked, still ashamed and surprised that they had not reacted before, but determined to watch for trouble now and glad to be doing something useful.

Jake was a rough-looking biker-type man with a long beard and hair yanked back into a neat ponytail; Coral said he was a good person but bad assed if needed. He looked tough. He stationed himself by the two, tied up men and glanced often at Marla. If anyone tried anything, he was going to break someone's arm real fast.

Jobie was the odd one out. He was a sixteen-year-old

African American, but Coral assured everyone that the boy was brilliant, dependable, from a great family, and well liked by everyone in town for his good manners and good nature. He grinned, despite the circumstances, proud he was included in the group to keep everyone safe and calm. He walked back and forth from the front to the kitchen and to the back as if he were on patrol. Coral said the boy would notice anything off-kilter quickly and would stay alert.

Annie, Lydia, and Dana moved between tables and the kitchen, delivering orders and filling cup and glasses. Despite the white tablecloths over the bodies with their red blossoms of blood seeping through the fabric, the two tied up men lying complacently in a booth, and a woman with no personality sitting at the counter, the diner seemed almost normal again.

Almost.

Chapter 10

Taps on the glass made everyone jump.

Pax looked to George and Dan to see what they thought before he opened the door to the two rain-slicked people outside; both were knocking to be let inside and gesturing to the door handle, but Pax didn't know anyone in town. No one could be sure who they were as they didn't lower their hoods, but George said he was sure the badges were real and that the glossy plastic-covered bodies were police.

With that part confirmed, Pax opened the door, and two figures came inside, shook off their umbrellas before they hung them up, and then carefully shed their slickers to hang them alongside the umbrellas.

Pax, Dan, and Jake readied themselves to fight if the two people were violent.

"You have a mess here," the woman said. She was dressed in the police department issued grey shirt, black slacks, and black books, and she patted at a mass of dark red hair that bounced in a heavy horsetail down her back. She wrinkled her nose as she looked at the tablecloths, covering the bodies on the floor.

Their whiteness blossomed in places with red flowers of blood. Gently, she pulled back each cloth, surveyed the bodies, covered them back, and then stood. She rubbed the toe of one boot against the calf of her other leg, her nose wrinkled as she took in the scene.

The State Police would have hell with the crime scenes all over town since they were far from secured, but right now, the danger was real and far from being over. At least this crime scene was dry, unlike many.

Ronnie reminded Pax of a nice, big red bay horse with her mass of red hair, sturdy body, and strong energy; she was tall and had sturdy bones. She was dismayed to see the diner in such a mess. "Whole family, unreal."

"This one is chewed on," the man in grey, her partner, stated. "And who are you?" He finished viewing the bodies and turned with a grimace, looking at Pax who was a newcomer to town.

Pax introduced himself and explained a little of why he was in town but saw the police officers, Ronnie and Mark, were not very interested. Mark had only asked for Pax to fill in gaps and because it was protocol.

Pax didn't care but told them, "That boy, this fellow over here, Myke, they called him, did that to him. He chewed at the boy and hid under the table."

"Myke?"

Pax pointed to the man who was tied up with strips of tablecloths and stowed in the same booth as was the tourist. "That's how they identified him. I saw it myself; he was eating that kid under the table in that booth," Pax gagged as he said it.

George repeated the events he had witnessed while Mark got himself a cup of coffee, and Ronnie asked for a soda. Both officers nodded often during the story as if it all made perfect sense.

"Aren't you gonna take notes?" Pax asked.

"I would if we had anything that made sense to put in the notes," Mark said.

"Still...."

"Seriously?"

"Ummm," Pax muttered.

"Every case tonight has been about the same: some person got wet in the rain, got violent, got calm. That's it.

It's best never to be around anyone who is getting out in the rain, but after he does whatever it *is* he does, he is fine if someone likes manikins. They just sit, stare, and do nothing. They're harmless after they finish their little anger outburst, not like they're gonna run away," Mark said.

"Murderers," Dan said, "guys, they killed that family under the tablecloths, and lookit Marla."

Ronnie shrugged and said, "I know, Dan. I know it's bad, but trust me, the killings are all over town. We have dead people in cars, in buildings, and on the streets; everyone has gone nuts. Right now, we don't know what to do but to tell people to stay inside and try to be safe."

"I saw Rick running people down," Gus said.

Ronnie and Mark looked at one another. "That explains why he didn't answer his radio," Ronnie said.

"I think it's the rain," Annie said.

Ronnie sipped her soda, looking at Annie as if she had said something very ordinary. "Of course, it is." People murmured around them, and Ronnie looked around at them to either side, her face a mask of confusion and surprise. "You didn't *know*?

Mark took up the conversation. "The rain came, and people went crazy, got violent; Doc says as near as he can tell...."

"Doc is working on this?"

"Of course he is, Annie; jeez, we aren't some back water town," Mark chuckled. "We took some of them down to the clinic, and Doc's been examining them, says he doesn't see anything outwardly, but in the brains...well...the ones he has looked at...the brains have just gotten all *smooth*. They don't have all the ridges and stuff like normal...whatever that means," Mark said.

"Like zombies."

"Zombies don't have smooth brains; they have viruses in their brains," someone else called out.

"There are no zombies," Coral moaned.

"I told you they're going *smooth*," Annie said.

Mark spoke up, "No zombies, that's ridiculous. It's some pollutant or something in the rain, maybe, and it messes with the brain chemicals and makes people violent as if they did PCP or something. After it wears off, there's no danger. It's all over town, but no one is a zombie. Jeez."

"So what is the plan? The cure?"

"We don't know," Ronnie nervously patted at her hair again. "Don't get wet, and then we wait until the rain stops. Meanwhile, we arrest the perps and clean up the mess and figure out what caused it. Rain or not, if perps hurt anyone, or if you know anyone who is hurt, then he is going to be arrested and tried for the crime. Business as usual."

"It isn't usual, Ronnie," Coral argued.

"Well, we're doing the best we can. Until it's daylight and the rain stops, this is the best we can do. Stay dry."

"Just like that?"

"Pax? Is it Pax? Okay, hey, we don't know any more than you do. Maybe there's something in the rain, like a pollutant causing the problems. We don't wanna panic people, but the State boys said these incidents are happening there, too, where it's raining. Doc is working on it, though."

"State boys?"

"State Police," Ronnie said.

"That's pretty crazy. So the bodies are supposed to just stay here?" Pax asked.

"I guess so," Ronnie said. "But you have it good here. It's warm and dry, and we can wait the rain out."

"Unless it rains forever," Dana whispered.

"Hush," Annie snapped. She tried to give Dana a frown, but the idea had crossed Annie's mind as well. What if it did keep raining? What was wrong with the rain?

She handed her friend a plate and told her to take it to a table in the corner. "Over there, Dana."

Eyes averted from the tablecloths covering the bodies, the patrons ate their food quietly, listening to the exchanges and what the police had to tell them, but every so often, they glanced back into the rain that fell relentlessly from the sky as the night pressed in closer.

Stress hadn't taken away Coral's ability to cook well, but the patrons only ate to keep busy.

It was full on dark, and the streetlights hardly pushed back shadows. In intermittent flashes of lightning, figures darted in the trees that dotted the park.

Coral slid behind the counter and poured hot coffee for Mark. "I'm gonna keep those two tied, and we'll stash them in the back room if you'll help me. I can keep everyone here warm, fed, and dry, and then everyone can head home when the rain stops. I'll do my part. If anyone comes in wet and crazy, Mark, I tell you if he does, then we're going to hurt him."

"You're within your rights," said Mark as he helped Coral and the rest take the two tied men to the back storeroom where they locked them inside. Mark told both men they were under arrest but received no response other than blank looks.

Neither man fought back but just looked at the men around them, unmindful of the sticky blood they had on their own hands or on the hard, concrete floor of the storeroom. Mark said that once they were this way, they didn't seem to get violent again, but Coral refused to untie the pair.

The fact was no one knew what was happenin'

Chapter 11

"Coral, my girl is home alone. I didn't get a sitter 'cause I am supposed to be off by now," Lydia said, pulling Coral to the side of the diner. "I'm really worried."

"Sam is alone?"

"Yeh."

Coral studied an empty cup before tossing it into a bin to be washed. "She wouldn't have called to go out into the rain, Hon. She's likely curled up and watching T.V., okay? Did you try to call her?"

"No signal."

"Chris wasn't gonna go by?"

"He's at the shop, tearing apart a motor; you know how he gets when he's working on a motor. I told Sam to order pizza, and I'd eat some when I got home. What if the pizza guy...."

"She's okay, Lydia. You have to keep yourself safe for her. When this rain stops...."

Lydia set her jaw. "I've gotta get home, Coral. I have to get to Sam."

"You can't go traipsing out in this rain. Maybe it's not the reason for all this insanity, but if it is...." Coral had lines of concern on his face. Lydia wasn't just a good waitress, but she was also like a daughter to him, and he was fond of her daughter, Samantha. He knew that Lydia meant to go check on her child. He thought Sam was just fine and that no one needed to go out in the rain.

"Gus, you'd let Lydia borrow your rain slicker and umbrella, won't you?" Annie asked.

"Why sure. Why does she need it? No one needs to go out in that. It ain't safe."

"She's gotta get to Sam and check on her."

"Oh."

Annie frowned. "Well, she can't go alone. I am not about to watch her go off alone with lunatics out there."

She turned to Ronnie and Mark who were devouring slices of apple pie topped with ice cream. They were members of the police force, and it was their job to protect and serve the community, but they didn't look as if they were going to get up and do anything.

Ronnie paused with the fork halfway to her mouth. "Now, Annie, come on. You called us 'cause you have a situation here. We can't all go running around in the rain and get sick and attack people. We're here working this crime scene."

"You want seconds of that *crime scene work*?"

"Please."

Annie thumped seconds of the pie onto their plates. The pie was good with flakey crust, covered with sweet filling and tart apples from the farmer's market across the street.

"I tell you what, Lydia, you can use Gus's slicker, and I can use Ronnie's, and we'll run to my Jeep. A little rain won't keep us down. And we'll drive out to your place and get Sam, all covered up, and bring her back here. It won't take but a few minutes to do it," Annie said. "I'm not letting you go alone."

Pax shook his head. "Not without me you aren't going. Officer Mark, if you'll let me borrow your slicker?"

"All of you can't go out there...."

Everyone begun speaking at once, and the buzz grew louder.

"Pax?"

"Ummm?" He was listening to the officers describe what they had seen out in the streets while he listened to Annie and Lydia make plans, but everyone in the diner was talking at once.

"Pax? You locked the door back?" Coral asked.

"Dan did. You did, right Dan?" Pax hesitated.

Chapter 12

"I...." Before Dan could finish his sentence, three wet dripping people barged into the diner, snarling and moving determinedly through the blood at the entrance way, without caring that they tracked it through the room. No, they weren't zombies, but they were wet, groaning people who didn't look normal anymore; they were determined to hurt someone. Anger and insanity filled their eyes.

A woman was barefoot, her feet were cut, and her sundress was torn and soaking wet; her hair was in strings about her face. With a staggering surge of energy, she jumped up and launched herself over a partial wall, right on top of the nearest table, sending dishes and glasses flying in all directions. She squatted there, looking at the people around her.

People screamed.

At the table, the couple and teen daughter had just finished eating as much as they had appetites for and were about to stretch their legs a little, walking about the diner when the crazy, wet woman banged onto the table in front of them.

They pulled away from her with shouts, telling her to go away. The daughter slammed a plate into the woman's side, fighting back, as her parents got out of the booth.

The woman dripped water onto the table and hunkered down, snapping her teeth at the teen girl. The plate crashed into the woman's nose, splattering blood everywhere; the girl, Carrie, almost fell as she slid out of the seat, grabbing her mother's hand. She had gotten a good punch in with the plate, allowing her to get away. "Mama," she called, dodging the wet woman's claws that reached for her hair.

"Get back, Daisy," the man and woman shouted, "what the hell are you doing?" The man threw a balled-up napkin at Daisy, angry for the mess she had caused and more than a little frightened by her behavior. Dishes and food were all over them and the floor. His daughter grabbed for her mother's hands, trying to avoid Daisy's wild lunges.

Daisy, perched on the table, canted her head to one side like a bird of prey and snagged a lone fork from the table; it was the only utensil she hadn't knocked to the ground.

Working at the only video store in town, Daisy would normally chat energetically to everyone who came into her store, and she knew this family well.

They rented a scary movie and a comedy every Friday night for their family time.

When the dad went out of town for work, the mom and daughter came in and rented seven or eight movies for the weekend, some romantic comedies and some horror movies. Daisy would always ask them what food they had planned and if they were going to get manicures, but she didn't talk now; she snarled and growled, brandishing the fork.

Unexpectedly, she leaped from the table to use her weight to push the teen girl, Carrie, to the floor.

Carrie threw an arm up and felt the tines of the fork sink into her forearm all the way to the bone. She shrieked. The fork hit the bone, slid, and went out the other side. Daisy lost her hold on the fork as Carrie rolled away. Carrie's father grabbed Daisy and lifted her off the floor before throwing her to the ground.

He kicked Daisy in her head. And it felt good to do that; he liked the sound and the feeling.

When she paused in the attack, he kicked again. Even when she was curled up and not moving, he kicked Daisy. He wanted to continue until her head and face were little more than pulp, but no one was really watching him anyway, so he lost interest. Had his daughter not laid a hand gently on his arm, he might have gone on kicking the woman forever.

But then again, the rain water from Daisy that had had soaked his arms when he was trying to pull her away from his daughter was dry, and he felt a bit better. The young girl's parents grabbed her to get her away from her attacker and behind the counter.

The man who had come in with Daisy was a ne'er-do-well who lived at the trailer park and cooked meth sometimes and sold it to make his money; he used as much as he sold.

Periodically, Ronnie and Mark rousted him. He was Bill, the

local drug addict and distributor, and he carried his own weapon: a brick that he used to bash at people randomly as soon as he pushed through the doorway; Coral ducked one way, and Pax grabbed Annie and Lydia to duck in another direction.

In his hand, the brick swooshed.

Trying to get the brick away from him, Ronnie dodged a blow but suffered a nasty scrape on the side of her head, making her dizzy while she cursed. Physical combat in a small town wasn't a daily activity. She could handle it, but it wasn't what she was used to. She thought that she should pull her gun and maybe shoot Bill, but in her years of duty, she never had pulled her weapon.

Mark slammed his gun down on the man's head hard enough to knock him out, and several people lay bloodied from the blows of the brick, so it was like a war zone. Mark was angry enough to hit the man a few more times but held back.

All the diners had jumped up to run but had scattered in all directions, so they tripped over one another and skidded on the rain-wet floor. A child screamed after flying to one side; a loud pop probably meant a broken arm. Her mother cradled her in a corner.

The third person who had come in was a man in his late twenties, big and brawny. He waved a big Bowie knife as he glared at the diners who were sliding and slipping out of his way.

In disbelief, an older man made a waving motion of dismissal at the big man because he recognized him and liked him just fine and then looked down at his stomach, groaning, his hands clutched at a spreading red stain. He was gutted.

The big man didn't seem concerned as he pushed the older man away and carried on through the diner, his head moving back and forth as if he looked for a certain person or specific type of prey.

Rain, dripping off his clothing, made the blood on the floor look pink.

A young woman in his path slapped at the dripping man who had come into their sanctuary, hoping to get some distance from him since she recognized the woman. She took a nasty slice across her palm but managed to half-slide under a table at a booth, her hand curled protectively to her chest.

Lydia screamed, "No. No. No." over and over as she watched in horror as her boyfriend, Chris, attacked all in his path, sent them running away from him or to the ground, bloodied and injured. He was the big man who had been the third one through the door, and his eyes seem to be searching for her.

Lydia covered her face with one of her arms, waiting for the knife to slice into her; Jake and Pax prepared to hit Chris with a tackle.

But something else happened first.

Chapter 13

Across from Coral's Diner in the other direction was the big Catholic Church with a tall steeple and stained glass; it was one of the oldest buildings in town, built solid and beautifully. After mass, parishioners watched a violent attack right in front of the church on the steps. In mass, they had retreated and called the police, only to be told this was going on all over, to avoid the rain at all costs, and stay dry with a group until daylight, and then the rain had stopped.

Some of the ladies had set up with cookies and coffee and iced tea and soda for the younger set. They used the kitchen to whip up sandwiches: tuna salad, chicken salad, ham and cheese, and cheese with tomatoes. There were chips and dip, and one of the ladies set out a salad and dressing.

Everyone had theories and ideas about what was going on that he shared or raved about, depending on one's view of what sharing was. Tired of the bantering, Joleen thought she would just go out into the rain and be done with it all. This was maddening to be stuck here.

Some said there was something wrong with the rain that fell relentlessly from the sky, but Joleen didn't believe in government conspiracies or that any aliens were testing them; that was all spook-talk and silly.

The younger kids were all suggesting that aliens had come down and poisoned the rain or that a giant alien was watching them like one would watch an upset, angry hill of ants. Some laughed and thought this was a grand adventure.

The older folks were trying to rationalize everything and come up with a logical reason for the sudden violence; one or two began speaking of an apocalypse, but most thought it was mass hysteria, but those who dismissed the worry and said it wasn't the rain causing a rash of violence still didn't rush out into the water to their cars.

No, indeed they did not, Joleen noted to herself. They all watched the rain, whispering and wondering, but didn't stick a toe in the rain.

They didn't *believe,* but they didn't *disbelieve,* either.

"Lookie, the police cruiser is over to the diner now, might be Ronnie...." That was Charles Williams commenting and pointing out the obvious. He was an African American man that worked at the big spa, making reservations and commiserating with the aches and pains of all who came there. He dressed in fancy clothes: a starched button-up, long sleeved shirt, silk tie {bought at a shop not in Cold Springs}, and crisp wool slacks every day of the year.

"I think Charlie is right...looks like one of the cruisers," Shelly Dulane said.

While Joleen waited for a chance to slip past those who were keeping them here in the church, yes, like prisoners, she occupied herself by fixing coffee and tea and plates of cookies for everyone. She patted everyone's arms in a motherly way and murmured that they would all be fine.

Her mind was somewhere else; the other day at Mildred's house, Joleen had done something so unlike herself, so very funny, that she still giggled to herself about how clever she was to have thought of such mischief.

While Mildred was in her bathroom with its fresh white paint, blue butterflies all over the walls, and a cute crocheted toilet and tank cover, Joleen took a bag from her heavy purse and exchanged three-fourths of the artificial sweetener with real sugar. There on the counter was a fruit gelatin box ready to be mixed for a sugarless treat that Mildred could snack on; Joleen exchanged the packet inside with one she had brought that was far more flavorful and full of sugar.

With a smile, she suggested Mildred go and sit on the sofa and relax and find some of the shows they enjoyed: where doctors always saved patients at the last second and had brilliant, perfect white smiles, and never wore anything but fancy duds. She prepared things for Mildred to enjoy all that day and the next since Mildred seldom went out. Jolene made a very sugary pitcher of lemonade and a strong, sweet kettle of tea and exchanged some cookies that she put on a plate.

Joleen wasn't sure what the sugar might do but knew that

Mildred was diabetic and wasn't supposed to have it. She poured mints into her handbag and from a zippered bag, added sugared ones in the little bowl; they looked just alike.

What a fine joke this was. She had been very angry with Mildred.

Joleen kept her hair long and tightly braided and went down to the salon to get a rinse put in every so often so that it didn't have that terrible yellow color.

At eighty, she was still very active, walking around the block each day and helping at the church. If she had had one regret, besides losing her husband of fifty years some ten years before, it was only that her false teeth were a little too big and made her seem wolfish when she looked into the mirror.

Joleen felt a wave of intense passion for doing her mischief.

Right now in the church while everyone discussed the rain. Mildred sipped a sweet cup of coffee that Joleen had made for her, making Joleen almost laugh out loud at her little joke. "I'll get you more when you want," she promised Mildred.

"You make the best cup of tea," Mildred remarked.

Joleen didn't know it, but she had a prank played on her as well, a terrible prank that would cause great heartache.

She would go home and find her precious silky-haired white cat, Penelope, with one leg ending in a stump, torn and bloody. Blood would be all over the floor and the soft white fur. The actual paw would be in one of the big rat traps Joleen kept in the attic for vermin but which was there in the middle of Joleens's pristine white kitchen. The cat hadn't really gotten a foot caught in the trap and gnawed its foot off, but the tableau was set up to seem that way, and Joleen would be hysterical.

She would say it was her fault: Penelope must have gone up and gotten into the trap, made it back to the kitchen, and then died while trying to free herself by chewing away the offending foot. Joleen would wail and berate herself for even having the traps in her home, but then she know who was to blame, and she would make him pay.

Charles Williams had set the stage himself, and because he wasn't an evil person or sadistic, he had killed the cat before removing the paw and setting up the prank on old Miss Joleen, putting one trap where it would have the biggest effect. His brain itched when he thought about what he had done.

When he went home, he would find they had been the subjects of a prank as well. *'Nigger'* and *'coon'* were written in black magic markers all over his house on Grande Street, scribbled on the front door, a pretty eggshell blue, and on the cream-colored siding. The offending words were written again in oily red lipstick and in something that was malodorous. The words would hurt Charles deeply.

No one had ever been rude to them, but they were two of the only ten black people in the whole town. People that Charles and his mother were around, such as their neighbors, were mystified by those who judged others by skin color. Charles never had felt even the slightest hint of racial discrimination. Had people been hiding how they *really* felt? Who thought that about them?

He would wonder who could have defaced their door that way. They would be outraged by the excrement rubbed into the siding of the home, wiped on the fabric of the seats and the wood of the rocking chairs on the porch, and mashed into the floorboards. Everywhere, they saw nasty, foul dog turds. And who had a dog on their street?

Bryce Landell.

Charles would recall how the man walked past their house every evening with his dog, Slugger that never seemed as friendly to Charles as he did to the rest of the neighbors. Was Slugger a racist dog?

Bryce Landell had been busy as well because he pranked Aimee Bright. Pretending to be someone else for a day or two on the computer, he had gained her trust and then had done something so clever and funny that it was almost too much to bear. {Periodically, Bryce broke into giggles for no reason anyone could see}.

A few years before, Aimee had been a cheerleader and homecoming queen, and now, seven years after high school graduation, she was just as pretty as a speckled coon dog with her long blonde hair, good skin, and perfect teeth and pretty blue eyes. She was a very pretty girl, and everyone knew it and remarked about it.

Oh, she was a smart one and worked at the library and had reading classes for little kids, and everybody liked her, but *she was too good*, she thought, *to date locals*. She was all over-stuffed about herself; she was full of herself.

Bryce might not have been much in the looks and charm department with his nerdy ways and big over bite and thick, coke-bottle glasses, but he was smart.

Aimee had a double whammy. Yesterday, while she was at work, he sneaked into her house and *smelled her panties and pillow, but we won't mention that part* in her bedroom (*where he felt the soft fabric of a burgundy satin bra that was glossy, cool, and slick and tossed to the floor*), he added a little juice from *Toxicodendron Radicans* also known as poison ivy to her face cream and hand cream.

'Leaflets three, let it be.'

And he added a strong hair remover to her shampoo and conditioner.

The rest was much easier. He simply set a program on the computer to bombard her email and Face Book pages with ads and web pages for weight loss and a site for *Fatty Chasers;* at a slim hundred and fifteen pounds, she worried obsessively about her weight. She would be assailed with images of fat women and suggestions that she should diet away the extra pounds.

Watching her there in the church as she worried about the rain and talked about it to everyone, Bryce chuckled, excited for her to go home and use the cream and shampoo and to get a bashing about her weight; it was just such a funny prank. Maybe it would make her less sure of herself and a little less snobby if she had doubts about her weight and a rash on her skin and excessive hair loss.

Beauty, meet the Beast.

Bryce worked at the pharmacy, and while it was true that sometimes he felt very nervous and sneaked a few tablets from a prescription, he did well at his job and gave people advice about their medications and helped everyone in town stay healthier.

Every day he grinned with his big choppers and wore the blue, calming pharmacy coat on his skinny frame (*his Adam's apple stood* out like Ichabod Crane) and helped his neighbors get their medication as prescribed and ignored the fact that some of the patrons snickered at him and thought he was unattractive.

Unfortunately for him, soon, he would have been the talk of the town as people found in the street or sitting on benches, leaflets that promised, "Cheap abortions, no questions asked, done in the back room under sterile conditions" with his name, the address of the pharmacy, and the phone number. The newspaper personnel would have come over and ask why on earth he wanted a quarter of a page for an ad for back room abortions.

He would have been furious at the prank, of course, and when approached by Father Tom, he angrily would have led the priest to the back room which Bryce hardly ever used and thrown open the door to show how dusty and unused it really was. Unfortunately, the prankster had hung a plastic baby from the ceiling and covered it with fake blood.

Bryce would have fainted and smacked his head hard enough to need a few stitches.

The little old lady down the street, Mildred, had used an old baby doll and bottle of ketchup for that prank, and a computer and copy machine were all one needed to pull a great joke on someone.

Aimee, who would lose her pretty golden hair and break out in a terrible itchy rash that would scar, had pulled her own prank on Drew, the man who had defaced Charles's home with dog poop.

She had slid glossy porn pictures into his sock drawer in the bathroom behind the soaps, in the laundry room on a shelf, in the garage, and between the mattresses, and Aimee had left Drew's wife a note in the mailbox saying that Drew was a porn addict. Aimee was on the Internet and Face Book all the time, and it was nothing to subscribe Drew to a ton of porn websites that would pop up in his e-mail.

Soon, Drew would also have gotten mail from companies

with samples of enhancement products, wild toys, ads for swinger's clubs, and more.

Aimee had finished by taking gallons of bleach and dosing his prized roses and miniature gardenias and azaleas.

If you asked each of them: Drew, Charles, Mildred, Joleen, Bryce, and Aimee why they did such terrible things, they wouldn't have an answer at all but would look blank and confused and claim it was a simple prank they had thought of. No one had suggested it to them.

Deep inside, Drew had always disliked Charles because...well...he was *black*. And Joleen thought Mildred made way too much of her medical issues; Bryce thought Aimee was a snotty bitch, and Charles considered Joleen a busy body in everyone's business. Drew was attractive, and Aimee might have dated him, but what did he do, he up and married that piece of trash from the trailer park!

The compulsions had worked their way into each person's head, squirming and digging for the little things that set each off, and once an action was taken, it was as if the itch were purged and cleaned, and then serenity began to set in.

They might not have acted as violently but would be as smooth as anyone else in a few days.

They were of the slow process.

Chapter 14

They didn't particularly recall the little shower, sprinkle actually, that had come up a few days before, barely dropping any water at all; Mildred counted a few drops that landed on her, making her hair frizz. Mildred and Joleen had been admiring Drew's roses. Aimee had closed the sunroof of her car as she backed out of the driveway with a half-hearted wave to buck-toothed Bryce as he picked up a piece of litter from his lawn. Charles and his mother sat on the porch, rocking, but Charles had been gathering the mail when the little drops fell.

Of the other two houses on Grande Street, one was empty with a cheerful **For Sale** sign on the front lawn, and the other was a corner lot that sided up to Hickory and belonged to Lydia and her daughter, Samantha, but neither had been outside at the time.

But that is what some of the people in the Catholic Church across from Coral's Diner were doing as both the night and the rain fell.

"God have mercy," Father Tom almost yelled as he watched the action across the street.

They could all see clearly into the windows of Coral's. Everything was happening at once: a woman jumped on a table and was fighting with some people, a man was swinging something at people, knocking them down, and a big, burly man {*who looked kind of like Lydia's man Chris, but he was a good man and would never do this*} was raising and slashing with what was a big butcher knife?

"That's Ronnie over there; she'll get 'em straight," a voice called out.

"Coral can handle it," someone said.

Father Tom said a silent prayer and drew everyone back into the church, away from the rain. No one tried to leave, but all talked about more theories.

Someone brought up Noah and his Ark; that possibility, that it was the end-of-time-flood that drew the older people and younger on the same side.

It might rain poison forever.

Chapter 15

Ronnie pulled her gun, and on the exhale, she pulled the trigger. Three bullets hit Chris in the head. She wasn't crazed by rain but just protecting the people in the diner, doing her duty.

Lydia screamed.

In Coral's Diner, people began scurrying to safety, to secure the violent maniacs, to bandage and calm those who had been injured, and to restore order.

Lydia stood and screamed hysterically, and Ronnie, her jaw open, looked at the man on the ground, whom she had shot and killed. Her blood was running cold in her veins.

Ronnie let her arm fall to the side and shook as she watched Chris bleeding out and listened to Lydia screaming.

"Now simmer down," Coral roared. The two police officers were useless as they looked to Coral for instruction. "One thing at a time."

Coral gently pushed Ronnie's hand down and helped her holster her gun. He ordered her to go to the counter, sit down, and drink some soda or coffee to combat shock. Like a child, she obeyed, and Mark took her arm to help her along although she cut her eyes to the side to watch Coral.

Coral went to Chris and checked for a pulse, shook his head, and sighed as Lydia cried harder. *Ronnie had actually made a fantastic shot, but she took no pride in it.*

Dan and George had the woman, Daisy, hanging between them as they carried her to the storeroom; sadly, the dead would just have to share space with the violent people. They tied up Daisy even if she did have extensive head injuries and was unconscious. They tried to feel sorry for Daisy, but she had used the fork to stab Carrie and had crossed over to being a criminal.

Jake carried the toddler to the back (Coral again noted the tiny Chuck Taylor sneakers), and then he carried the little girl to the back, her blonde pig tails with the blood dried to sharp little points. Jobie helped with the woman and then with the partially eaten teen boy. They laid the bodies in a line and covered them with the diner's tablecloths. Each of them looked sick after having to move the pitiful bodies to the back.

Bill, who had barreled in and wielded a brick at people, was still out cold from where Mark had bashed him in his head, but they tied him up as well.

Coral noted that the back room was now full of dead people or murderers who were hogtied. Pax laid the man down on his stomach, his hands secured in Mark's handcuffs, and shrugged a little at Coral. "His pupils aren't the same size. I think the cop hit him pretty hard."

"Well, he shouldn't have been hitting people with a brick."

"I agree."

"Nothing we can do but defend ourselves."

"If we can. When we can."

Chapter 16

The town nurse, Marnie, had set up a triage station with help from Annie and Dana, using the diner's first aid kit and some make shift supplies they had found. Cloth napkins made clean, soft bandages and slings. Vinegar was fine to wash with. The older man with the slice to his belly died quickly and was put into the back room while his wife sat at a table with others and cried softly. Of the rest, the worst of the injuries were a broken arm that Marnie wrapped lightly and set as best she could, and a few nasty cuts and scrapes that she coated with cream and gauze but that would scar if they didn't get infected and kill the patients.

A make shift triage and vinegar weren't a decent substitution for real medicine and real doctors and nurses.

Carrie's parents were both suffering from light shock. Her mother, Susie, was able to talk and follow instructions even though she was cold and pale, but Carrie's father was distant, uncoordinated, and more confused. He wasn't able to tell them about how wet his arm had been with rainwater.

The tines of the fork had slammed right into the bone of Carrie's arm; the wound was painful and needed to be watched for infection but wasn't serious.

Marnie used the cream and bandaged her arm, telling her that she would have to take antibiotics to make sure she healed without becoming infected.

Lydia sipped hot tea and shivered beneath the tablecloth; she and Ronnie were both suffering mild shock.

Marnie's main patients were three people who had suffered when Chris, Lydia's man, had come through with a huge Bowie knife. One patient needed to be in the little hospital that Cold Springs had, and although it wasn't fancy, it was big enough to give the young woman antibiotics, something for pain, and suture deep cuts on her hands and arms. The immediate concern was two long slashes, one along the woman's neck that had missed the artery but still bled heavily and gaped at the edges. The other was a long cut from the woman's temple and across her cheek and was so deep into the chin that Marnie had to keep the section of flesh in place with gauze and a lot of tape. Finally, Marnie wrapped the woman like a mummy from the neck to hairline.

The second wound was a slash into the belly of another man Chris had tried to gut. The knife had nicked the stomach itself so that digestive fluids leaked out and burned, causing incredible pain. Marnie was unable to relieve the pain, so she stuffed cloths close to his belly and allowed the man's wife to hold the bandage securely.

Lydia was the third patient that Marnie worried about. While she had suffered only a slash on the palm of one hand, Lydia was shivering from the shock of seeing her long-term boyfriend on a murderous rage.

"Breathe slowly," Marnie ordered.

"That wasn't Chris."

"I know it wasn't."

"It looked like Chris," Lydia said, "but it didn't *do* like him."

"He'd never have attacked anyone," Marnie said. She patted Lydia's arm. "His mind was gone, Honey."

Annie held a cup of hot tea for Lydia to sip.

"Just drink it. It'll help," Annie snapped. She knew it didn't taste very good, but it was very strong and had sugar and lemon, so it would help.

"Why would Chris…Ronnie…she…."

"Ronnie had to. That wasn't Chris. He was soaking wet and sick with whatever is in the rain. You know that, Lydia."

"He was sick."

"Ronnie had no choice. You have to be strong so that we can go get Sammy."

While Marnie had patched up patients and the men had removed bodies and the culprits to the back room, Coral locked the doors and turned the lights way down low so that the front was dark. Maybe no one would know they were in the diner.

"How's Chris?" Lydia asked again, probably the fifth time.

"Lydia, we talked about that," Annie said again, worried about her friend's mental state.

Seeing Ronnie unholster her weapon and fire into Chris's head had been the most horrible thing they had ever seen. Ronnie was curled up in a corner, shaking; she had never had to fire her gun on duty, much less shoot anyone. And she had killed a man she knew and liked.

"He's dead. He was sick," Lydia repeated.

"And you have to focus," Annie said.

"I've gotta get to Sam," Lydia said again.

Annie petted Katie as the dog ran from person to person, presumably checking on each. "Okay, you and I will go. Here, pet Katie. Katie's worried about you."

Lydia did as asked, rubbing the dog's fur and then hugging her while Katie licked Lydia's cheek gently. Amazingly, Lydia's face began to take on more color, and the terrible shaking abated. Annie had heard that petting animals lowered blood pressure and helped a person's health. She would get Ronnie to hold Katie next.

"We will go," said Pax as he interrupted, "I'll run for the Jeep and pull right up next to the back door, and you two jump in. When Lydia is feeling better,Lydia, you have to get your shit together, or we're not going," Pax said.

"I have to get over to my mom and dad's place," Dana said. "I can run for my own car, but maybe we can all go together."

"What is about to happen is everyone in here is about to panic and decide he needs to be somewhere else like cats, all of a sudden, bolting out of a room, running. And when that happens, we'll have wrecks and mistakes, and it's gonna end badly." Coral came over, speaking low, "I'd offer my Explorer, but it's a bad plan if we all go running out into this rain."

Lydia didn't know how to explain that getting to her daughter was far more important than Dana's mission to get to her parents. The man with the stomach wound groaned, reminding Lydia and Dana both that he and a few others needed to get to the clinic quickly.

"Are you doing okay?"

Annie grasped the hand Pax laid on her shoulder. "I think so. Wow, I guess you picked the wrong time to come visit me, didn't you?"

"Imagining you here alone...I mean without me...no...that's far worse. I'd rather be here and doing what I can. Annie, I'm gonna do everything I can to get us out of this safely," he paused. "I picked the perfect time to be here with you."

"I'm sorry you are suffering through this, but I am selfish, Pax. I'm so glad you're here with me. I'd be scared out of my wits without you." She meant it. [She wanted to say much more and hear him say how he felt, too, but the situation didn't work out, as they wanted}.

He looked around a little dramatically, giving her a chance to back out, but she still kept her gaze on his eyes, and he leaned in to kiss her. After months of chatting, the reality was as perfect as he had imagined. He hated to break the kiss. "Love you lots," he said, just as he had said every time they logged off the Internet, but this was in person.

"Me, too. Love you lots." She was about to say something else. Probably as sappy, but Pax had his head cocked to the side with his eyes bright and flashing.

"Grab pencils, as many as you can."

Chapter 17

Annie looked at him as if he were crazy, and she chuckled, "That's romantic."

Pax grinned and patted Katie as she ran by him. "I have a weird idea, but it might work."

"What?"

Pax motioned Jobie over to the butcher's block to get a big piece of butcher's paper. "Can you draw an outline of the town? I need the blocks and streets, and make 'em true to size to each other and give me the names. I need to know how long the blocks are, so add the squares for stores or whatever; get some people to help you if they're good at drawing. I need details and details."

"I'm on it," Jobie said, grinned proudly.

"We can plan to get people to the hospital, but I want to see it: the town and how it is laid out."

Pax spoke quickly, describing a crazy idea he had to George and Dan and Jake. The three men got it at once as only men can who are apt to build off of structures. "You want a big ole open box with a giant upside-down, squared off U shape at one end, hanging way out, and yeh, that could work." They began sketching and arguing as they worked.

Pax gathered supplies with Coral's help. The other men excitedly built what Pax had envisioned, and after they looked at the simple open-ended boxes, they said they were perfect.

"We have to weigh them down back here to offset that over-hang." It was just that: a big open box, but at the far end, they had an over-hang that would give them cover from the rain. It was junk and wouldn't hold up long, but they only needed it for a short amount of time.

"What is that thing?" Annie asked, "are you making a fort to play in?" she grinned at Pax.

"Imagine we set it right outside under the awning in the back and you walk into the box; that over-hang is gonna keep rain from blowing at the sides and from pouring off the top so that people can get into vehicles."

"We can staple some big trash bags on top."

Annie looked at them, flummoxed, "You big idiots. You have to keep it off of you totally. That means in the car, too."

"So we stay wrapped in plastic. Once we're wherever we're going, we strip it all off. We can get new bags; people have trash bags. Shower curtains...think outside the...ummm...box." Pax looked at the structure they were nailing and stapling together.

"This is the most idiotic idea I have ever heard," Annie said, "someone has to run for the cars. I said I would go with Lydia. You don't have to make it...all this."

"We have to keep you safe. You can't stay dry unless we prepare."

"Gus did it. He used a slicker and umbrella and stayed dry, and he's sane, right?"

"As sane as Gus has ever been," Coral said.

He walked around, checking on Marnie and her patients and looking over the front of the diner which was dark and locked up, but if someone wanted inside badly enough, he could use a brick, bash in a hole, and climb inside.

Even though they had moved the attackers and the injured and the dead, blood was all over, tables were on their sides, plates, food, and silverware littered the ground, and it would take a lot of scrubbing before the diner could be reopened.

Maybe he was selfish, but Coral felt sad for his diner and would hate to be out of business for the days it would take to clean everything up after the investigation.

"I should get the car," Dan said.

"It's my slicker; it won't fit your big ass." Gus covered himself again as he had before and took Jake's keys to his big SUV.

In a few minutes, he pulled the vehicle right up to the weird box that Pax had made. Dan and Jake helped Marnie load the little girl with the broken arm into the car, her mother, the man with the stomach wound, and his wife (all covered in trash bags taped together), and three more with cuts and scrapes. They worked slowly, alert to even a drop of water that might fall from the sky.

Gus got back into the driver's side by scooting over so that he didn't get soaked again, and Marnie slid into the passenger side, crinkling with baggies from head to toe. She cracked her window.

"How do you feel?" Pax asked.

"I feel normal. Sweaty in this, but normal," Marnie said. She asked each of the passengers and got the same response. "I think we're okay."

"Gus?"

"Feel like myself."

"No worms in the brain? Itching...weirdness?"

"No more than normal." Marnie shrugged.

At the hospital, a nice dry over hang was at the emergency room, and they could unload there while staying totally dry. "Good luck, guys."

They waved Gus and Marnie away.

Pax watched them go and looked at Annie, "Our turn, and I think the rain is a little lighter; let's get covered, and go get Lydia's daughter."

Part Two

Chapter 1

Annie taped the legs of the pants she made for Lydia from a black trash bag. Lydia already wore a top with the plastic tight about her wrists and neck and a plastic hoodie over the top that draped down. There was only a small slit to peek out from. Pax and Annie wore the same suits. "I could be a fashion designer," Annie said.

Under the baggies, Annie had a little fanny pack with more tape and baggies. Dana adjusted her hood and then reached over to help Dan cover himself fully. The five planned to go check on loved ones and bring them back.

"Katie," whispered Pax as he knelt to look into her eyes, "you know Coral, and he's a good cook and a nice man. I'm gonna come right back, but if anything goes south, would you take care of him for me? He will need you for protection; you can do that, huh?" Pax swallowed hard.

Coral looked at Pax and gave him a slight nod and told him, "Katie will take great care of me. Don't worry about us. We'll hang together."

"Thanks." Pax rubbed Katie's head, hoping his eyes would clear of the teary blur fast. Coral would take care of her if he didn't make it back, but there was still a lump in Pax's throat.

"We'll be right back, Katie, beautiful girl. You could go, but we have to keep you safe. Okay?" Annie sniffed.

Had Pax not already been crazy about Annie, he would have fallen in love with her right then as she reassured his beloved dog.

When Dan ran for his big Bronco, he slipped on the gravel, teetered for a second, his arms wind milling, and his friends held their breaths until he righted himself and went on. Had he fallen and torn the plastic, he might have reacted to the rain, if that *were* the cause of the aggression.

He pulled around under the new over-hang. The others piled in and fell back against the seats in relief. Pax said they should wait a few minutes and make sure they were all still okay and not dangerous to the rest.

"Feeling aggressive? Angry?" Dan asked them.

"Nervous and scared," Lydia said, "I'm dry."

"All of you feel okay then?" Coral asked them. He was almost shaking with nervousness. "Annie?"

"I feel fine," she said.

Dan pulled out of the parking lot with a thumbs-up signal to Coral, and they got a better look at the town. They could see up and down Main Street through the rain, and it looked as if there had been a few wrecks.

"Pull in there. It's dry under the side, see?" Annie pointed Dan towards the church across the street. "We need to check on them. They're looking out at us."

Her words were lost as Dan pulled into the intersection. A terrible, rocking thud hit the Bronco, and they thought a car had crashed into them, but a man was screaming and beating at the driver's side glass with both of his fists.

His mouth was drawn back in a snarl as he roared and slammed his hands into the glass. They knew this man: He was Isaac, an old man who haunted the streets, dug through trash bins, and slept where he could find a place. Homeless by choice and always refusing help, he roamed the streets of Cold Springs, and this night, he was soaked by the rain and was full of fury.

Rain twinkled on his faded beanie hat and tight grey curls of hair. {The town's people treated Isaac almost like a favorite pet}.

"Oh, my God," Lydia shuddered, "go; go."

"Isaac...." Annie let her fingers trail down a window, as she looked at the man, mild by nature, usually harmless, but now violent.

Dan stared another second at Isaac's angry face and then pulled away so that the man fell onto the road behind them. Dan looked in the rearview mirror and saw that when Isaac picked himself up, he headed down the street towards the river, watching for movement that indicated there was someone he could take his anger out on.

Father Tom met them in the driveway of the church, avoiding the water, speaking to them as Dan lowered his window a little. They traded information quickly, and Dan warned them not to go into the rain.

"It's dangerous out there."

"Keep everyone here until the rain stops for good and the ground dries a little. Keep everyone calm, and let each know that some of the police are handling things," Pax told the priest. "If someone attacks, you'll have to fight back. A lot of murders have happened tonight, Father."

"We'll be on guard," said Father Tom as he let Annie introduce him to Pax; then, he nodded. Annie had shared with the priest that she liked a man she spoke to on the Internet.

While he had been a little skeptical and protective, Father Tom hadn't criticized Annie. At least the mystery man was staying calm, was being helpful, and was brave.

Father Tom listened to some people behind him who were speaking up, and although he argued with them, he relayed that two of the people in the church were asking to get a ride to their neighborhood.

The young priest might have ignored the pleading and soothed them, but the two who wanted to go along lived exactly where Lydia lived, on the same street. He shrugged.

After a few whispered comments, the people in the Bronco said they would take the two along with them but couldn't be responsible once they were dropped off. They had to scoot over and crowd in as two of the parishioners prepared to go along.

"They have to cover up," Pax explained to Father Tom, "head to toe with bags and tape. We have water on us, and they can't get wet." He regretted that they had come over here now. The more people with them, the more chances for problems.

Some of the people grabbed bags and tape and went to work on the two that would ride along. Both looked strange in the shining plastic.

Miss Jolene was an older lady and worried about her cat, Penelope. She lived on the same street as Lydia. Charles was the other who crowded in; he was concerned about his mother being alone, and he, too, lived on Grande Street.

"Penelope is fine, Miss Joleen. She stays inside, and besides, we don't know if animals are affected," Annie said. She began wondering if animals might go mad as well and had a vision of a pasture of cows becoming angry and racing at them in a rage. *Mad cow.*

Chapter 2

At 3rd Street, they turned right at the grocery store. The lights were on, and the store was torn apart, the plate glass was in jagged pieces on the parking lot, cars were tangled into metal puzzles, and a truck had rammed right into the front door.

Dan drove slowly, and they were able to see inside where boxes, cans, and bottles were tossed onto the floor, displays were ripped apart, and cashier stations were torn and smashed. Dark stains that were probably blood covered the store.

"Looks like a bunch of people had a hell of a fight in there," Pax noted.

"I don't see anyone moving or anything," Dana said, peering through the window. "That's probably a good thing."

Earlier, people coming into the store, had been rain-soaked and had attacked those in the store who were dry, chasing them down aisles, throwing cans, and smashing and slicing with whatever weapons they could find.

The dry people fought back but were no match for those infuriated with blood lust. After the effects wore off, those who had maimed and killed looked about the store with no interest or concern and wandered away.

"How do you think it feels?"

"What?" Annie asked Dana.

"Getting that rage and then going smooth?"

"Ed...that guy...said it was like worms in his brain, itching," Annie said.

Pax nodded at Annie's words. "It must feel like going crazy and being angry, and wanting to hurt people and then feeling itchy, I guess."

"And then nothing," Lydia said. "Ronnie didn't have to do that. Chris would've been just nothing but not mean. He would have mellowed out, but Ronnie killed him," cried Lydia, again.

"That wasn't Chris any more. Chris wouldn't hurt a flea. Lydia, you know he would be horrified and disgusted to walk around like...well...like Dana said...a zombie."

"They aren't zombies," Pax said automatically.

"They're empty. There's nothing left...like it burns out. No, Chris wouldn't wanna be like that, Lydia," Dan added.

Charles gasped, "Ronnie shot Chris?"

"Well, he was stabbing people," Lydia cried into her hands.

Pax and Annie shook their heads to indicate to Charles not to ask any more questions about it. "It was just very bad. We don't know how long the calm lasts or if there's another stage or something else. We don't know anything about this."

Dan made a left onto Hickory, and they all felt panicky as the water on the road rose dangerously high. In a while, the roads would be flooded, and the rain would come into cars, trying to get through. Involuntarily, they raised their feet although the water wasn't coming inside.

"The river area may be flooded, Dana," Dan warned, "we won't be able to get down there if it is."

"Hickory is always flooded; we can do it," Dana argued.

Pax gripped Annie's hand.

Dan turned right, and they were on Grande.

Dan went down the street, circled in the cul-de-sac, and came back, pausing at Charles's house. Despite the rain and darkness, they could see the graffiti someone had scrawled all over the door and siding. "*Coon*" and "*Nigger*" were written clearly.

"Oh, my God, Charles," Dana whispered, "that's horrible."

Charles made a little whining sound but then told Dan where to drive so they'd be closer. He was whispering the hateful words to himself over and over like a chant. Charles jumped from the Bronco, slammed the door as he waved to the rest, and ran to his home, calling for his mother.

In October, as a trick, kids might soap windows or toilet paper a house, but destroying property with graffiti wasn't common at all; in Cold Springs, kids pulling a stunt like that wouldn't be able to sit down for a week, would have to scrub the words off and repaint the building, be grounded half a year, and pay off any expenses by working. Children here were brought up the old-fashioned ways, for the most part, and parents didn't spare the rod.

Dan felt for Miss Joleen, his elder, but not enough to run around in the rain for no good reason. After telling her his plan, he got close to her porch, and she gingerly got out, keeping her baggies close about her, and went inside.

"She looks so small even in baggies," Dana said.

Dan and Pax cursed a little as the Bronco almost got stuck in the wet lawn and mud, but then the vehicle roared like a beast and lunged forward. The steering wheel spun in Dan's hands, and the Bronco shot out of the mud onto solid ground. Even in these circumstances, they cheered. Dan grinned, "That's my Bronco." He stayed in one place a few seconds to let the adrenaline settle.

In fact, they were cheering and laughing with relief so much, they didn't hear Miss Joleen. Going into her home, she immediately, carefully removed the baggies, all still dry and dropped them onto the floor. She went to her pristine kitchen for a drink of water, calling for her cat while she patted her hair into place. My, wasn't she tired from the evening's events? But finally she was home safely.

There on the white floor was her Penelope, lying in a pool of blood, one precious little foot seemingly gnawed off; the cat's mouth and whiskers were bloody. Joleen stared at the scene for a second, thinking it couldn't be real. It was too awful to be real.

A huge rattrap, like those in the attic to catch mice, rats, or squirrels, lay in the room and was snapped close; in it was one of poor Penelope's little white (now red) paws. The cat was stiff with death; Joleen took in the scene and looked at all the blood, opened her mouth, and let out shrill scream after scream.

Joleen thought about how earlier, she had noticed something about Charles and asked him about it, curiously. Charles had small scratches all over his arms and face but claimed he had gotten into a thorn bush. Then, she had no reason not to believe him, but were they cat scratches? Maybe.

Gritting her big teeth, she looked down at the floor closely and thought she saw little curly hairs that, yes, could have been from anyone; right there next to Penny's muzzle, weren't those a few nappy hairs from that boy?

Joleen was livid. Charles had wanted to come home, too,

not to see his mother as he said, but so he would be around when Joleen found Penelope. He was a sadist.

Across the street, Charles' mother didn't greet her son as he came in. Had she not been concerned? Had she not been hungry for the two entrees he was bringing home? Charles yanked away the baggies and tossed them to the side as he went room to room, looking for his momma.

Finally, on the front porch down on the boards, she sat, not making a noise behind the banisters covered in ivy. "Awe, Momma, did you see what they wrote?"

Mama looked up calmly. "I caught him. Ran out there in the rain while he wrote on the house and got that critter. He can't write it no more." She didn't seem upset but explained with no emotion.

Her words hit Charles like a sledgehammer. "You went into the rain?"

"Sure did."

Charles knelt and saw what was left of Drew. Most of him was slopped into a messy wheelbarrow, hacked by a big hatchet that sat beside his mother on the porch. Each of Drew's fingers had been split down the center, each nail had been ripped away, and the nail beds had been stapled. Finally, each tip had been burned crispy black, and Charles somehow knew the arms and all had been attached when the pain was administered.

His sweet, loving mama, who tended injured birds, was as gentle as an angel. She had stepped into the rain, caught the prankster writing things on the siding and door, and had done this to him; Charles didn't understand how she could have.

Charles sat in a small puddle of rainwater that his mother had dripped onto the porch, feeling a rising anger over this entire mess: the relentless rain, his mother's uncaring attitude, and the dead, mutilated body in the wheelbarrow.

Across the street, Joleen had gathered her evidence as to who had killed her beloved Penelope, and she burst out her front door, screaming his name. "Charlesssssssssssssssssssssssssss." She was already hurt and angry before the rain touched her. "You killed my Penny, you rotten *nigger*."

Now, she was beside herself with fury.

Charles looked up sharply. What had she called him? Was she insane? He had worse things to worry about than Miss Joleen right now; his mama was burned out, and there was nothing left of her personality and, well, Charles had a mutilated body on the porch. How inconsiderate was this old bat?

"Get back in your house, old Lady," said Charles who was upset and worried for his mama. "Get off *our* yard."

"Whoever wrote that is right, you nasty little *coon*. My daddy used to coon hunt; the bitches were mean." Joleen kept walking, her face a mask of fury. She dramatically waved a fireplace poker as she walked though the rain.

In the Bronco, everyone stared out the window; all the yelling and movement in the rain had stunned Dan so that he didn't drive away. They could only watch as the action unfolded before them.

"Shut up," Charles yelled.

"*Coon.*"

"Get off my yard." Charles hefted the hatchet and without thinking, bolted down the walkway. "Go on, you crazy old bitch." The rain felt warm as it covered his skin, warm and heavy, like a weight pressed against him. Why had they feared this? It was wonderful. It was much better than the little puddle he had sat in; this was amazing.

Charles felt strong, fast, and angry.

"*Dirty Coon.*" They met In Charles's yard, and for an old lady, Joleen looked tough and ready to fight. She smacked the iron poker across his arm and chest something fierce before he could say another word or react.

Charles felt raw indignation and a rush of fury; who was *she* to name-call and come into *his* yard and hit *him*? It hurt, too. For an old woman, she hit very hard.

He brought the hatchet up and slammed it down on her shoulder so that it all but severed her right arm. Blood splashed all over her, and as he raised his arm back, blood fell onto his shirt as well. *That would teach her a lesson.*

Joleen backed up a few paces, shocked that Charles had

done that, and then she snagged the poker with her left hand and ran at him, sticking it right through his chest. It was stuck for a second but then slid right into Charles.

Watching, his mother hardly blinked. She had no cares in the world.

The combatants on the soaked lawn tussled a few seconds, but the hatchet was lodged firmly in Joleen's shoulder, keeping her from fighting as well as she would have liked. The pain blazed enormously in her arm, shoulder, and up into her head as the nerves screamed.

Had the blade fallen out, blood would have flooded down her arm, and she would have passed out, but the blade held some of the vessels closed.

Joleen kept pushing at the iron poker, shoving, driving it deeper into Charles, and he howled with pain, wondering how the pain could keep getting worse.

When the poker was shoved in all the way to the hilt, Charles made his big move, his final move. He lunged at Joleen, grabbed the hatchet, and with all his strength, yanked it back, causing her to stagger forward and the poker to shift, making every organ and nerve in Charles roar with agony; blood rushed out in a crimson sheet, running down the old woman's arm. Charles managed to lift the hatchet over his head and slammed it right into Joleen's skull.

Both collapsed into the falling rain; the fury and anger slowly were replaced with complacency and a Zen-like calm. There, in the mud of the yard, both would slowly bleed to death, but neither cared, for neither feared death nor struggled against the pain.

Joleen and Charles lay in the rain and accepted death calmly. A philosopher might expound on the fact that both Joleen and Charles had been infuriated but had cared much less than one normally would about the pain they suffered. They didn't die with fear and dread, clouding their minds, but with peaceful acceptance.

Some people might say that this was best, not to fight death but to let go. Poets might say it was best to fight and not *go gently into that good night.*

Although it was raining and dark, everyone in the car watched the battle across the street, wondering why it was happening and why the two people sank so peacefully into the mud.

Dan and Pax almost jumped out of the Bronco and went after the pair to stop the fight, but the angry people had weapons that would rip the baggies and possibly stab them. Dan kept saying that he couldn't believe Joleen was using a fireplace poker on anyone.

Dana thumped the car seat with frustration, wondering how Charles could chop at an old lady. "We could get them now; they're down."

"What if they aren't finished and they use those on us? Whatever this is, they have it," Annie argued. "We don't know what happens *next*." She buried her face for a second against Pax's shoulder.

"We have to go do something...." Dan started, but he didn't finish his sentence as he saw them sink into the mud. The fight was over. How could they risk themselves if everyone in town were acting this way?

Annie rubbed her face, and Dana sniffled back tears.

Chapter 3

"I just need to get to Sam," Lydia reminded them of why they were out here. "Can we just go?" {She was as selfish as she had to be in order to get to her child}.

Dan put the vehicle back into drive and drove to the end of the street where Lydia lived, on the corner of Grande and Hickory. The houses there were older homes, with three and four bedrooms, two or three floors, not enormous, but roomy and well kept. They had been re-done over the years, and most had siding or were neatly painted, had modest yards filled with large, old trees, roses and flowering bushes, and lush lawns.

Some years before, most families had added garages that would open up to the houses via doors. Lydia pushed a button on a pad in her purse, and the one-car garage door rolled up so that Dan could drive inside. Lydia led the way, and Pax, Dana, Annie, and Dan got out of the Bronco, sighing with relief.

Annie got Lydia stripped of the plastic, and Lydia opened the door. Carefully, Pax stripped the bags off of Annie and the Dana so that they could also go into the house. Lastly, the men yanked away the coverings, took a last glance around, and slid into the house, locking the door behind them as Lydia lowered the garage door.

Like most of the homes, Lydia's house had old, wooden floors that gleamed with wax and were covered here and there with rugs. Ancient wallpaper had been stripped so the walls were covered with smooth paint and wainscoting. Here was a stone fireplace, there was a stained glass window, and over there was a tidy built-in shelf of knick-knacks. A small, but beautifully redone kitchen and a dining area with a bay window were nearby.

"Sam? Sammy? Baby?" Lydia's voice cracked with emotion. By feel, she went in, felt for matches, and lit a small candle that smelled of peaches. The little light helped chase away some of the darkest shadows.

There wasn't an answer.

"Sammy, Hey, it's me, Annie. I'm with your mom, and we came to get you. We are perfectly dry. Can you hear how normal I sound?"

"Baby? Come on, baby, come to Mama, please...it's safe...."

A small pajama-wearing figure darted down the stairs, paused to look at her mother's eyes, then slammed into her arms, crying, "Mama...."

"I'm here. I came as soon as I could. Are you okay? Talk to me now," Lydia sounded a little stronger now that she was holding her daughter in her arms.

Sammy raised her head. "I'm okay. I was scared though. I hid."

"Good. That's my smart girl."

"Uncle Chris came by, and he beat on the door a while, but he sounded mean and mad, so I didn't say a word."

Lydia wept harder. "You did the right thing." Chris, in his fury, had been here, first, trying to get her baby? Lydia's stomach dropped. "You did the smart thing."

Annie rubbed Lydia's back, knowing how close of a call that had been; had Chris gotten in, he would have killed Sammy.

"It was on the Internet, Mama."

Pax scooted closer. He saw Lydia shaking. "Annie, can you get us drinks? Let's sit here a second and get our heads clear." He smiled kindly and said, "Hi, Samantha. I'm Pax, Annie's friend. I came all this way to meet her, and boy, did I pick a weird day for it. I met Annie on the Internet. Can you believe it?"

Sammy peeked at him. Her mother slipped to the floor to sit next to her and gave Sammy a nod to say Pax was an okay fellow, but then Sammy had believed Uncle Chris was okay as well until tonight.

"Sam, or Sammy. That's what people call me."

"Sammy, you knew what was going on? What exactly was on the Internet? We haven't heard much."

"Not a lot. People, at first, it was like a joke that everyone was doing...saying that it was raining and that everyone who got wet, got mad, and hurt others. They made little jokes.

But then people got scared and said it was true, and some of the news places talked about the rain. Everyone was posting things...horrible things." She began to cry softly as Lydia stroked her hair.

"Is it...just around here in Cold Springs?" Pax asked, confused, wondering what Internet sites the girl might have looked at and how reliable they were.

Sammy shook her head and answered, "No."

"Is it like part of the state?" He watched her shake her head. "No? Is it in Texas and Arkansas?"

"More."

Dana made a choking sound and went to help Annie. Dan sank into a chair, dejected. "More? My God, Sammy...."

Sammy wiped away a tear. "Before the Internet and T.V. went down, it was raining in California and all across the map and also was starting in Florida and going all the way to Maine. They said it was an Emergency State."

"They declared a State of Emergency?" Pax asked. Sammy nodded. "You are doing awesome at giving us the information, Honey. I have a few more questions for you, okay? Because so far, you have been the best of all at knowing anything...better than the police."

"I have?"

"Oh, Honey, no one has had nearly this much information, and we have been just wondering and worrying," Lydia added.

"I can try," Sammy said.

"Did anyone mention the National Guard?"

"Yes," Sammy tried to think, "they are trying but have to stay dry, too. No one knows anything that has been said." She looked terrified.

Pax thought he should change tactics and that the lack of anyone in control and working on the problems was very frightening, not only to Sammy, but also to all of them. "Did they have any advice?"

"Use oil to keep it off of your skin, and don't get rain on you. Ummm, protect your self, and either hide or fight back. I hid."

"That was smart."

"As soon as it stops, we can begin to put things back together. But stay at home, and stay dry. The DCC said...."

"CDC? Scientists and doctors? They talked smart and fancy?

Used some big words?"

"Yes. Them. They say stay dry, and this has gotta be a pollutant from a passing star or junk in the sky but could be something leaking out from here or a terror-something."

"Act of terrorism?"

"Yep, That is it. I knew that. Like the tower thingies got run into with airplanes. They said it could be that without the planes, you know."

"Okay, so they don't know much," Pax smiled, reassuringly. "Big heads never know much; they just pretend to, Sammy."

Sammy finally gave Pax a half-smile. "They did sound silly talking over each other. They said it will pass, the rain will stop, and things will be okay. People always say that. How is Uncle Chris? Have you seen him?"

Annie and Dana brought in sodas and snacks.

Pax glanced to Lydia but saw her tighten her eyes and sink a little. He cocked his head. "Sammy, you are sharp and solid, and I respect that. I am going to be straightforward with you, okay? Chris must have come here first, and you were very smart to hide. He had the sickness that's in the rain. It makes people angry and violent, you know that. They aren't themselves anymore."

"Uh huh."

"He left here and came to the diner. We didn't have the doors locked or know to hide like you did, and he came in and was pretty crazy acting. He had a weapon, and he didn't mean to, but the rain made him hurt a few people.

Do you know Ronnie, the police officer? Yeah? She's pretty cool. Well, she had to disarm him, that means to make him drop his weapon, and he was back at Coral's, and all of the violent people were locked away." Pax didn't lie. He just left out parts in his explanation. Lydia gave him a silent *thank you* with her eyes.

"Oh, okay," Sammy said.

"We came to get you, Honey," Lydia told her daughter, "and we can go back where Uncle Coral is, and we'll all be safe. You love his cookies."

"I'm tired," Sammy said.

Pax nodded, "Me, too." {No, he was exhausted, not sleepy,

but bone-tired}.

Lydia had some rum put away to go with her soda, so she was more steadied, but she was also yawning, now.

Despite Dana's worry about her parents and her demands to go check on them, she began to doze off in a chair from exhaustion, and when Lydia told her to go lie down in the bed, she did so without arguing.

"Go; get some rest, and take care of Sammy. I can stand guard a while," Pax told Lydia. Annie said she would help him, and Dan finally agreed to nap for a little while before he took over as guard.

Lydia cuddled up to her child in her room, and they fell asleep. After everything that had happened and despite losing Chris and seeing what he had done before being shot and even though it was raining, the world was falling apart, and everything looked hopeless, Lydia had her daughter with her, and that was enough.

"Go sleep. I'll stay on guard," Pax said to Dan. "I'm wide awake. He went through the house and checked on the locks on windows and doors, pulling the drapes closed and turning off lights so the downstairs was dark.

It was the first time he and Annie had a chance to talk normally, and she wanted to know about his trip to see her and why he had decided to surprise her.

He only smiled when she stopped asking questions and slipped off to sleep. Covering her with a soft throw he found at the end of the sofa, Pax watched her sleep; at times she mumbled and looked afraid, but then her face would soften, and she would sink deeper into dream land.

Pax knew that beyond a shadow of doubt he was in love with Annie; she was the woman he had waited to meet and be with the rest of his life. Unfortunately, he was concerned that he had waited far too long to meet her.

Chapter 4

Coral didn't think it was precognition or anything worldly that made him start planning something different than what they had thought of before. A few random events and observances ignited him into action. Immediately after Dan had driven away in one direction and Gus had driven in the other, Coral and the rest heard a thrumming in the front of the diner.

Someone that they didn't know, maybe who was in town for the spas or sight seeing, was outside one of the windows banging his fists against the glass. A man snarled and glared while he beat at the glass.

Someone behind Coral whispered that this man had already tried the door, and after finding it locked, he had begun to hit the window. The glass was thick, but if the man grabbed a brick or something to break the glass, he would get inside and attack.

With the entire front almost all glass, it might be only a matter of time before someone broke in.

With the lights out and the lightning intermittently flashing, Coral had seen Dan drive to the Catholic Church. As he drove over, a homeless man they all knew as Isaac, had run at the Bronco and tried to get inside but had fallen as they sped away.

As much as it scared Coral to see that, he figured the incident had terrified those inside the Bronco. At the church, it looked as if someone or a few people climbed into the Bronco before it took off again.

Gus was already down 2nd Street and had presumably turned on Pine to get to the clinic to help the patients he carried.

As Coral watched, a trio of figures joined several others in the rain, and they resolutely walked toward the well-lit church.

One man carried what looked like a baseball bat, and a few others carried things that Coral couldn't make out.

He wanted to warn Father Tom or to help, but he could only watch as the people in the rain walked to the doors and the windows of the lobby area and raised their hands and arms. It was only a few minutes before the people climbed through the broken windows, and Coral didn't think he could hear screams from where he was, but he could imagine them all the same.

"What are they doing?"

Coral jumped as Ronnie whispered to him in the darkness. "I think those are crazies…messed up with the rain…Rainies, and they are going after the people in the church."

"I need to do something."

"If you go out, you'll get wet and be part of the problem. If they corner you, they'll rip you apart, Ronnie. The church is big; maybe most can hide." Coral walked past her and softly called Jake, George, Mark, and Jobie to him. "This is what we need to do…." He outlined his plan, explaining what he had seen at the church.

Mark looked to Ronnie, wondering if they needed to go help. If they did, they would leave these people unprotected.

"And do what with it?" Jake asked Coral.

"We'll have to bug out. We can't stay here. I'm wondering if Annie and Dan made it. I don't know that Gus even made it." Coral got everyone's attention.

"Dan is reliable, and that guy, Pax, he seems okay," Mark said grudgingly. "I think he's pretty sharp. The gals are dependable too, and no one is gonna keep Lydia from Sammy."

Coral nodded. "I can't make you go; you can stay. But I am leaving, and I hope you'll go with me. We aren't safe here. I want to load supplies up: food, water, trash baggies and table cloths because that's what we have here, and then get some vehicles and get across the bridge and out of here. We can drive out and go where the State police and others can help us. We'll get Lydia and the others and Gus, and next, we'll get out."

"Just leave our homes and the town?" a woman asked.

"I think we have to for now until the rain stops and someone can figure out what caused this and if we can make the place safe again," Coral said.

"We're gathering stuff; come help us," Jake ordered.

"What the hell?" someone said. They heard rumblings of a big engine.

Chapter 5

Coral motioned them to continue, and he walked over, suited up in baggies, and went under the over-hang to see what the new arrivals wanted. It was one of the Cold Spring's school buses, one of the only two the town had. When the door opened, Ben peeked out and said, "Hi, ya, Coral."

"Hi, Ben. What are you doing?" Coral was a little surprised at how folksy they both were speaking and suppressed a grin.

"Got a few with me; they are all okay, got them down at the firehouse and hotel. I ran for the bus and loaded them up, and here we are. Figured you'd know what to do, and there ain't no one at the police office, now."

"That was mighty brave, Ben. I guess you saved their lives. Mark and Ronnie are here."

"Awe, someone had to do it." {He was proud someone had noticed}.

"That's all you found?"

"Oren," Ben said, "he said we had to bug out." He pointed to the patrol car parked behind the bus. Oren, the chief, waved at Coral and blew a kiss to Ronnie.

"Why'd you come here and not get out of town?"

Ben clucked, shaking his head of grey curls and slapping the steering wheel once, lightly. "You didn't hear the commotion? Coral, the bridge went."

"Went? Went where?"

"Gone. Down. Away," Ben said. "It's gone. The river flooded: covered the trees, and flooded the bridge which fell in, and now there's nothing much left. I can't tell in the dark and rain, but near as I can tell, there's really nothing left."

Coral felt sick. That bridge was the only way out of town.

"We aren't safe here. We saw some of the 'Rainies' go after the people in the church across the street, so we are grabbing stuff to bug out. We were going to leave town after we find Annie and Gus and the rest."

Still in their slickers, Ronnie and Mark listened. None of the rain came into the overhang, but they were still jumpy about the rain. Ronnie blew a kiss back to her father as he waited in his cruiser.

Ronnie pointed.

Behind the bus was the other police officer on the small force; he was Oren, the chief, and he waved from the cruiser to hurry and get a plan.

"Oren is with us, I haven't seen Rick, and Oren couldn't get him on the radio, much as he tried."

"He's gone smooth," Ronnie said.

Ben seemed to understand what she meant. "Let's load up your people and stuff, and we can get out of here if we figure out where to go."

Dressed in baggies, everyone handed out boxes and containers of supplies. Coral had plenty of food, *and if he could feed the masses, then he would. Give him a fish and a loaf of bread, and he would feed everyone who hungered. This was what he was meant to do,* he thought.

He motioned to Oren and hoped the man understood his gestures and pantomiming, but he had a lot to communicate. Ronnie laughed and handed Coral her radio as she said, "I should have just let you keep waving."

Coral chuckled and spoke to Oren a while. He explained what Gus had said about the fourth officer, Rick, running people down, and Oren took it hard, hating to hear it, hanging his head for a second, and then Coral filled him in on all of the rest. Ben gave up more details.

Ben had explained more to Coral, Ronnie, and Mark. The bridge over the river had been bashed by huge, uprooted trees, and maybe worse, it had crumbled under the assault of rocks and slabs of concrete, breaking and rolling into the river, pieces of the bridge tossed like a child's blocks.

The river was running hard, way up over its banks as was the small lake that the river traveled through. Lake Road and the picnic areas, all the grounds, and everything around the river were under water.

It was the worst flood ever to hit the town, even worse than the one back in the 1930s that had done so much damage. But that had been before levees were reinforced and the river had been allowed to go freely through the lake.

Back then, the farmlands had drained, the river hadn't come up even close to the school or courthouse, and the town hadn't been in danger of washing away.

How they would get supplies and come back from this, Coral didn't know. Economically, the storm was destroying the town, and the massive violence wasn't helping.

After making it though this alive, the towns people would have clean-up and sanitation issues, homes and businesses would be ruined, people would be left without homes or jobs, many people would have some to mourn and to bury, and if the crime scenes were viable, criminal cases would have to be cleared.

Children would miss school, and the farms wouldn't be fit for growing anything. But if all pulled together, they could rebuild. Maybe they would need FEMA, like those people had needed after the hurricane in New Orleans. But they needed help now, if they were to make it through *this* rainy night.

"The hotel, both spas, the Methodist Church, the bar and gas station, parking lots, and streets are several feet under.

I'd say the houses on lower Hickory and Willow are flooded, too, and the trailer park is flooding as we speak.

I didn't see anyone driving out of there either, so all may be hunkered down, waiting for this to blow over," Ben winced as he spoke. At least twenty homes, twenty mobile homes, and a dozen businesses were involved in that.

He didn't mention what might have happened to any who were camped near the lake; there were usually half-dozen campsites in nice weather such as they had been having.

In his mind's eye, Coral could imagine people struggling against canvas and nylon tents, getting tangled in aluminum tent poles, and being washed away with their supplies down the river and off to the south, only to bog down in the swampy area of the lake.

"We need to get to one place, somewhere we can defend, but also be comfortable in while we wait this out," Coral said. "That's what Oren says."

"I'd be comfortable in my own bed," Ben grumbled.

"Yep, and when a few of these nuts knocked your door in and stabbed you, would you be comfortable?" Coral asked. "We're safer in a group. But where?" {He didn't add that one of the violent nuts could be one of them if they got wet}.

Ronnie frowned. "I would normally say we should go to the court house and stay there...."

"But that's about to flood," Ben told her, "already you'd be wading in at least two feet to get there, and I don't think you'd want your feet soaked."

"And the school is always a rally point."

"Flooded, too."

Ronnie rolled her eyes at Ben. "The highest point in town is Main Street Hotel." She had learned that in school when they were taught about the town.

"It's in the center of town, too. A little kitchen is there, along with plenty of beds. With supplies, we could hole up there for a long time," Coral agreed, "good thinking, Ronnie."

"Ben, you take the bus and get under the portico. None of the Rainies can get in the bus really; it's like a tank. I am heading down to the hotel to look for other survivors and Dana's folks. Ronnie, take Jake and George in the cruiser, and I'll take Katie and Jobie with me; then, we can go together.

While I do my rat killin' at the hotel, you three can start loading up guns and ammo at the station to take with us. Oren says to do that." Coral felt he should add that part so that they would know he wasn't the only one making plans. "We'll come back and help, hopefully with some more people."

Ronnie nodded. "It's a plan. Ben, be careful out there."

Coral called back into his diner, "Who's got that fine motor home out yonder?"

"That's ours. Mitch and Sara O' Donnell."

"How about this: You two drive it to the medical clinic, get Gus and Marnie and others who can help you, and get the injured loaded up. The situation may not be so comfy, but you need to get all of them to Main Street Hotel, too, where they'll be safer, 'cause there are way too many windows and light at the clinic."

"That's a plan. 'Bout time we got to help," Mitch O'Donnell said. He and his wife smiled. They looked to be in their forties and eager and ready to work. "We'll get everyone we can from there and then come on over. I doubt one of those...what are you calling them? Rainies? Those Rainies can't fight with my big 'Bago."

"Do what you have to if they try to attack you. You know...defend yourself," Coral said. "Ummm...Oren...."

"Gotcha. Oren says defend ourselves." Mitch nodded with a smile.

"I'm ready as soon as we get it loaded up," Sara added, "I'm gonna run for it; Mitch, your knee might bum on you."

"Now Sara...."

"Don't you get me going on my being able to out run you," she said as she looked at Coral. "I still run every morning, and I ran track when I was in college, so I am the one going. Get me taped up in my baggies, Mitch."

Coral turned, "Oren says, Mark, you go with them for security, and take a couple people with ya; bring back a lot of supplies, ok? You're the tough one, Oren said that, too."

" 'Kay," Mark said. He knew that he was an adequate officer, but that Ronnie, Oren's daughter, was the star of the police force. "I'll keep them safe."

"I know you will." Coral gave him a pat on the shoulder.

Mark nodded as he continued to put more supplies on the bus, alongside the rest.

"Oren says he is ready to drive out to Lydia's, see how they are and bring them back. He says any dry ones he finds on the streets can come. We need someone in one more car to follow Oren and be there in case he needs help. The roads are bad, and no one needs to be out alone." A man and woman with two teen kids, none of whom they knew, offered to follow Oren in their van.

A family of three was huddled in the break room, and they were terrified to go out into the rain. Coral hated to leave them all alone, but they would have food and items they needed and could stay there if they wanted.

He thought it was a bad idea to stay, but that was just a

feeling in his gut, and he didn't know anything for sure. He wished them the best of luck after warning them he didn't like the idea of leaving them behind.

Katie whined as she looked at the family and looked to Coral as if she were asking him to make them go. She didn't want them to stay behind, but they had made up their minds. With her ears perked up, Katie followed Coral.

"What about the violent people?" Ronnie asked.

Coral spoke to Oren again.

"He says to leave them tied," Coral said, "he says we have enough going on without dragging around a bunch of crazies with us, and he doesn't care who it is."

"Daddy, I had to shoot Chris. He's dead. Over," Ronnie spoke into her radio now that her father could hear her and the reception was clear.

"Was it by the book? Over," Oren hesitated only a second before asking her the question.

"Yes, Sir. Over."

"Sometimes the job sucks, Ronnie. I'm positive you did things by the book and had no other choice. I'm sorry you had to do that; there's nothing worse than having to take a life, but keep your chin up, and we'll get the town settled; then, you can tell me what happened, okay? Over."

"Yes, sir," she answered, "let's hurry this up, okay, Daddy? Over"

"You got it. Oren out."

Coral patted her back and flashed Oren an *okay* sign with his fingers.

It was a raggedy-looking group that pulled out from the diner, some dressed in baggies and trash liners with many loaded onto the school bus; behind the bus came Oren's cruiser, Coral's Explorer, Ronnie in the other cruiser, and last was the big RV.

Coral wasn't sure why, but with a chief of police and two officers, he was the apparent leader, yet he took it in stride. If this were his road, then he would walk it as best he could.

Chapter 6

In the big bus, Ben only had to turn onto to 2nd, then immediately back onto Main, and a few doors down to Main Street Hotel's portico. He would wait there for the others sure no one could get to them and attack.

Oren drove the same way but continued down Main to Farm Road so he could bypass most of Hickory. The van followed. As he passed the houses at this end of Main, Oren noted most homes were lit up and several had windows broken and front doors standing open or broken open, canting sideways. Light filtered out onto porches as rain drizzled into front hallways. It looked more like a war zone than anything else. A figure darted around a house and across the street ahead of Oren's car, but it was too quick for Oren to see who it was or where the person went after crossing.

He made a right turn and looked at the corner lot; its fence was bashed in and trees and a swing set wrapped around a car. It looked as if the Miller's son's red *sports car-go crash,* as Oren always called them and thought of them, did *go crash.* Hadn't he asked, "Now, Jim, why'd you wanna get that boy a *sports car-go crash*?"

Just as Oren was about to make the left onto Grande and a right into Lydia's drive, an explosion behind him caused him to slam on his brakes.

In the T where Farm Road met Hickory, the van carrying the family of four was hit broadside by a car before the van could turn. That car had to have been *flying* south down Farm Road because the heavy van skidded for a second and then flipped over as the ram bar on the police cruiser hit it. It wasn't a sports car, but it had gone crash for sure; it was a police car.

The Crown Victoria stopped in the middle of the T.

" Damn," Oren hissed, sick to his stomach. His father had been chief, and his grandfather had been chief, and Oren was chief, and one day his daughter would be chief. But damnit, there were days when he wanted to sit down and curse his profession for a good long time and then just quit.

Most days the job was nothing more than being a visible

presence or chasing along some rowdy tourists, telling some kids to get their clothes on and to move to another place to park and neck, or telling some of the kids to move along and stop bothering people.

Once in a while, there might be a shoplifter or a few drunks raising hell or a loose bull running down the road, but they didn't get trouble like this.

Oren's bad days were cursing the bull and yelling at the drunks and wondering why city kids came around, causing trouble. He had often followed teenagers to the bridge, warned them not to come back over, and asked himself why he went into law enforcement.

Oren tightened the slicker around himself, checked the extra baggies, set his hat on securely, and prayed for the courage to get out of his Crown Vic and go assess the damage. He thought of how brave Ronnie was and cursed himself a few times before opening his car door.

He unsnapped his holster strap, his gloves making it awkward.

Oren avoided the deeper-looking patches of water on the road and watched the other cruiser. Rick, the fourth officer on his force, got out of the cruiser, unfolding his tall, thin frame. He wasn't wearing a slicker or bags and was messy and damp looking.

"Rick?"

Rick stared at the van a few seconds and dragged his gaze towards Oren. He didn't respond verbally, but he seemed aware of his boss.

Oren unholstered his Colt Python and pointed it some where in front of him but not at Rick yet. "You hit them with the car."

"Did I?"

Oren noted a bundle smashed into the ram bar and cracks in the windshield, laced with gore that the rain hadn't fully cleaned. He knew what Coral had told him. "I guess you did. Have you been running people over, Rick?"

"I guess. I don't know. Maybe." Rick let the rain pour over him, and he leaned back against his ruined car as if he hadn't a care in the world but was here for a nice conversation. [About the weather}?

"Why the hell are you running people over?"

"I don't rightly know."

"You're about a dumb ass, Rick. Did you know that?"

"Okay."

"Dumb as dirt."

"Yes."

God have mercy, Oren thought.

"Rick. I want you to take your cuffs and cuff yourself inside the cruiser and sit there. I want you to stay there. You do that, you hear?"

"Okay." Rick stood straight and reached for his cuffs. The rain poured down his face, and he didn't brush it away.

"Wait; set your gun down first, and kick it over to me. You know how I want you to do it."

"Sure." Rick casually took his gun with two fingers and dropped it into a shallow puddle. He used a boot to kick it, clattering and splashing towards Oren.

With his gun trained on Rick, Oren watched Rick curiously. The man he had worked with for the last twenty years would have been almost dancing with nervous energy, pulling at his hair {And he always needed a haircut, and didn't Oren have to bitch about *that* all the time}, and cursing a blue streak over the crash. The jittery behavior was gone.

In Rick's eyes were recognition and maybe a faint recollection of his life, but there was no interest at all. No anger, no fear, no emotion remained.

Oren carefully got the handgun and set it on the back of his own car. Rick opened the car door of his wrecked cruiser, got inside, and complacently snapped his handcuffs on his wrists.

"Why did you hit them?"

"I wasn't paying attention. I was watching."

"Watching what?"

"The rain," Rick said.

Those two words chilled Oren. He kicked the door closed and noticed that Rick sat there in the driver's seat and would not move an inch until he was told to.

He thought Rick had been violent earlier and run people down, but this had been an accident since Rick didn't seem to care about anything, now. He hadn't been really thinking as he drove along the road too fast and with blown-out headlights. {He kind of wished Rick hadn't had his legs in the cruiser so that when Oren kicked the door, it would have bruised the man's shins, but that didn't happen}.

When Oren finished being angry about what was wrong with Rick, he would be sad and would mourn the man who used to be.

Oren was way too old to climb around on a rain-slicked van, but he managed to get up onto the side since part was crushed. The window was broken, and rain pelted the interior of the vehicle. Carefully getting his flashlight out and aiming it, Oren looked into the van. "Hey, Hey, are you okay?"

The man was missing from his seat, and his wife was crumpled in the passenger seat, wedged against the broken window on her side. Oren knew she had died when the van flipped since she wore no seatbelt and was flopped over in a boneless-looking way. Her face and head had bled a lot.

As he maneuvered the flashlight farther back, Oren saw the man had been alive after they were hit, had disengaged his seatbelt, but had been dragged into the back by his teen son. Maybe the man had intended to try to help his family or to get away from the rain.

The boy's face was terrifying in the small light. Somehow, the boy had become soaked with rain and dragged his injured father to the back of the van where the boy killed him, or maybe they had fought. Probably both. The boy had been a nice-looking kid, but now his hair was wet and frizzed and his eyes feral; he was hissing and snarling like an animal would over a fresh kill, warning Oren away.

The boy's lips and teeth were blood covered as were his hands, chin, and chest; he snapped at his father's neck where he had already opened it up and ripped at the flesh with teeth and fingers. No longer moving, the father lay on his back while the son dug at his father's throat, and his blood poured out. It was a pitiful sight that Oren knew he wouldn't soon forget.

If the boy made a move towards him, Oren would shoot him deader than dog shit. Oren shook and struggled to get himself under control.

Before he pulled his light back, a slight movement caught his eye. There was a soft whine. "Someone down there?"

The boy snarled, clawing at his father's eyes as if he were rooting for something deep within the sockets or the brain. Oren thought again about shooting the kid, and if he licked his fingers or ate anything, Oren was going to fire. Some things were not to be allowed.

"Please, help me," At the edge of the light, a teen girl cried as she peeked up at Oren. She was mostly covered with boxes and bags that had scattered everywhere inside the van. Her face was scratched, but her eyes looked sane and very afraid.

"What's your name?" Oren asked, keeping the boy within his sights.

"Amanda. Mandy," she whimpered.

"Hi, Mandy, I'm the police chief here in Cold Springs; I am here to help you, okay? Don't worry, we'll get you out of there fast," Oren reassured her.

"Uh-huh."

"Are you hurt?"

"I think some bruises. My head hurts a little," She said as she turned sad eyes to Oren.

Oren took a few seconds to think about this problem and how he was going to get the girl out and to safety.

He had a crazy idea, but with the state of things, it hardly mattered how outlandish his plan was. "Mandy, I'm going to get my umbrella and some tarp so we can get you out without your getting in the rain. You stay back there, and don't get wet, okay?"

"Uh-huh. The blanket is wet."

"Push it away slowly with your shoes. Very slowly."

Mandy pushed at a sodden mess of rags and adjusted her position. Her brother growled and snapped, but the agitation seemed less violent than it had been; however, she still jumped and made a soft keening sound until he looked away from her. "Please don't leave me," she cried louder.

"I won't. I'm going to get that stuff, and I'll be back fast. I won't just leave you. I have a daughter named Ronnie. Did you see her back at Coral's? She was the perky red-headed cop? That's my Ronnie."

"I saw her. She's pretty."

"Yep, takes after her momma. God rest her soul. Ronnie is a good cop. Mandy, she's smart and patient and notices everything. She can get a little lazy, but you know how that is."

Oren could tell the girl's heart rate had slowed a little, and she was listening to his voice. "You stay still and quiet. I want you to count slowly and see how long it takes me. Let's see, can you start at a one hundred twenty? Go backwards. Go slow 'cause I'm an old man." {And my, didn't he feel twice his age right now with his joints aching and his body exhausted}?

"One hundred twenty." Pause. "Hundred nineteen…."

Oren slid off the side of the van, almost falling into the water and breaking his neck. {What would happen to the girl then when she was finished counting}? He caught himself and concentrated on walking quickly but carefully to his patrol car. A glance to the other car reassured him that Rick hadn't moved a bit. Oren grabbed an umbrella and a tarp he had tossed into the back and one more thing he knew he needed.

At the other car, he took a huge breath. "Rick, get out here. I need your help." Oren was more than a little angry at the situation.

"Okay." Rick climbed out, and Oren uncuffed him. Perps always immediately rubbed their wrists where the cuffs chafed, but Rick didn't. He didn't do something as simple and universal as that. He kept his hands down. The behavior was so out of the normal that Oren paused for a second, puzzling it out. Rick not only had no emotions, but he didn't care about himself or anything around him either. Everything was *fine*.

"We're gonna use the umbrella and tarp and keep the window area dry for that girl to climb out. I want you to stand on the side and hold the tarp up so she has cover. Got that, Rick? You don't let one drop get on her."

"Okay."

Oren wanted to scream at the man. Rick normally would have been excited, would be asking a hundred questions, and would have been nervous as hell, but he was little more than a robot, now. Oren never thought he would be missing Rick's endless energy. He wanted to punch Rick until his teeth broke and eyes puffed black and purple.

Oren ordered Rick to boost him up onto the van, hating the man's hands on his slicker, but it was easier to get up there. Next, he told Rick to climb up.

Again, the teen boy snapped and hissed, protecting his kill. He had dug fingers into his father's eye sockets more and torn off the eyelids so they lay against the man's cheeks like fat, red tears. Oren gagged and called out, "Mandy?"

"Seventeen. I made it to seventeen," she said accusingly.

"But I'm back."

Oren told Rick to hold the tarp over the window, and Oren used a gloved hand to knock glass away so the girl wouldn't get cut. Oren, explaining to Mandy that Rick was what Coral had called *Rainies,* began to make plans. "Mandy, we don't have a lot of time. If we wait, you will get wet and turn into a Rainie. Now, I am gonna be giving orders, and you can either follow them, or I will not stay and help you. I can't help if you don't do everything I tell you when I tell you." {He was going to try, but if she didn't do what he said, then, yes, he was going to leave her to her fate because he had more things to do this night}.

"Okay."

"You cover your face and look away; curl up and away from your brother, okay? Do it now." Oren saw Mandy did as he said. Barely hanging on to the top and staying on the outside, Oren had to stretch as he brought around the heavy tire iron he carried. With all his strength, Oren slammed the tire iron into the boy's head several times, poking, hating the noise of the wet thud and groaning of the boy. In a few seconds, the boy's head was a messy pulp, and he lay next to his father, unmoving. {Maybe he was dead, but maybe he wasn't}.

Mandy whimpered; she knew what Oren was doing.

"Mandy, stay as dry as you can, and don't touch things unless you have to. Get up. Okay. Now, what you're going to do is take my hand and pull yourself up here. The tarp will help, and I have an umbrella, too. There's some wet spots but keep going, and we'll dry you as soon as we can."

Mandy was thin and small in stature, so Oren thought he could pull her up. She whimpered as she saw her father and brother but did as she was told, taking Oren's hand and kicking her legs up to climb. Oren pulled her upwards.

Mandy's whimpering faded, and her eyes began to fill with anger as she struggled to pull herself up. Her other arm was clamped onto Oren's arm like a vise. With a huge surge of strength, Oren yanked her up to the edge and through the broken van window so that she was on the side beside of him, but she was tossing her head and hissing at him.

His stomach in knots, Oren realized that his glove was soaking wet with rain and that was what she was clinging to. Mandy growled at Oren, angrily raking a hand alongside his face. Oren punched her in the stomach so her air whooshed out; she sagged. Oren took the tarp and wrapped it about her and slung her over his shoulder.

"Rick, you get down, and help me to the ground. I'm gonna be carrying her, so you have to take all my weight and lower me down."

"Okay," said Rick as he climbed down.

Tossing the umbrella to the ground, Oren slid to his butt and waited until Rick was in place to help him.

Rick reached up and pulled Oren down gently and sat him on his feet. After ordering Rick to follow and get into the back seat, Oren put Mandy into the passenger seat, sliding the handcuffs onto her wrists. She rolled her eyes, barred her teeth, and moaned, but she didn't act out anymore. She was somehow caught halfway between being herself and being violent.

Chapter 7

Oren didn't have far to drive. Telling them to stay in the car, Oren parked in Lydia's driveway, hoping that after all of this, they were there. He beat on the front door, announcing himself.

Pax asked a few questions and opened the door, ready to fight if the man were violent, even if he were the chief of police. Looking at the man in the slicker and trash bags in front of him, Pax wondered why he was out in the rain.

Oren, asked for Lydia. Pax felt his head spin for the next few minutes as Annie awakened. The man that Annie said was a good guy, brought in a snarling, angry girl who was like a damp cat, fussing and hissing and a soaking wet, skinny, tall man that Annie said was named Rick, a police officer. Pax remembered the others had said he was out running people over with his patrol car.

Lydia and the rest came downstairs, saw the situation, and came back with their arms full; she threw towels at Rick, telling him to dry himself. He undressed as told to, and using rubber gloves, Lydia tossed the wet uniform into her dryer with a distasteful look on her face.

"Why'd you bring him?" Annie asked.

"He held the tarp pretty well," Oren said, "he isn't violent now, he's...."

"Smooth," Annie said.

"Yeah. I don't know what to do with them."

It was hard to imagine Rick had been helpful because while Rick followed orders and exhibited no interest or emotions, his actions were losing grace rapidly. He fumbled with the towels and often stopped drying himself, staring blankly, until he was told again what to do.

"Are you okay, Oren?" Lydia was watching him as she asked.

"Not fully."

Dana paused and looked closer at him. "What's wrong?"

"My brain kind of itches...."

Pax's head jerked up, and he looked at Annie. Her eyes had gone wide; she remembered that guy, Ed, said the same thing. *'My brain kind of itches.'* If Oren started spouting about *'Spaghetti in his cake'* and *'frogs in the bugles,'* Pax was going to grab Annie and run.

"What do you mean?" Lydia asked him.

"It makes me want to yell and throw things, but I'm okay; I can beat this," Oren said quietly, concentrating on keeping the itching at bay. He sipped rum and Coke that Dana brought him and looked at a wet patch on his pants, up near the thigh. "I kind of felt better when I took care of that kid. I had to help her get out, or he would've attacked her, but I didn't really mind doing it."

"Oren, you need to fight this and keep who you are. Stay focused," Dana said. "You know you can do it. You didn't get much rain on you, maybe a bit at some other places, but you aren't soaked."

He took a towel and dabbed at his pants, drying the fabric. He ran the towel over his hair and feet just in case he had gotten wet. "I'm okay," he said, wishing he could open his head and scratch at his brain.

Pax looked out the window, peeking from behind the curtains. "It's getting daylight." In a weird way, it almost surprised him since he had kind of expected never to see the sunlight. The rain still fell, and the yard was like a pond, slick with water. It was impossible to tell where the street ended and where the yard began.

There was nothing but water as the entire street flooded where the old lady and young man had fought. {What was the water covering, now? How many bodies}?

Pax told them they needed to pack up and get out. "I think we're sitting ducks right here with nowhere to retreat if we're attacked."

"It's still raining?"

"Yeah. It comes down hard a while, and I see lightning, but then like now, it's just a drizzle, but it hasn't totally stopped yet."

"Will it ever stop?" Sammy asked.

"It has to. It'll stop sometime," Pax said, "let's get ready to go."

Lydia and Sammy packed the most important things into the Bronco, and then they added food to help with supplies at the hotel.

Sammy kept casting curious glances at Mandy who rocked back and forth as she sat on the floor close to the front door. The teen kept rubbing at her hands and arms, moaning and rolling her eyes with rising agitation. "She keeps doing that," Sammy said.

"Yes. It's unnerving, isn't it?" Lydia asked, rubbing Sammy's back.

"I guess she doesn't get that she's dry. Her arms and hands are where she was wet," Oren said, "I wasn't thinking when I pulled her out, and she got them wet."

"No, she wants it back," Sammy said, shivering, "look at her eyes."

Oren frowned, "Mandy?"

The teen rubbed harder at her arms, waggling her fingers in the air, and shaking her head, "My head...."

Sammy must have seen something because she stepped behind her mother quickly and squeaked just as Mandy jumped to her feet. Oren involuntarily rubbed at his revolver, ready to draw it. Dana grabbed a candlestick, and Pax pulled Annie behind him as he prepared to fight back.

Instead of attacking, Mandy whipped her head to the side, making her hair fly; she grabbed the doorknob, handcuffs clanking, and turned it, opening the door quickly, and leaping out into the rain.

Dan made a movement as if to tackle her but stayed in place.

Mandy ran across the porch and jumped into the pooled water on the lawn. It was up to her knees, and she flew outward to fall into the rainwater, face first, soaking herself. At first, she let out a groan of pleasure and then split the air with a bone-chilling howl. She drew herself out of the water, looking back with a hate-filled expression.

Lydia slammed the front door and bolted it just as Mandy hit it with her body, smashing at the wood with tight fists. Her back to the door, Lydia bent over, gasping, "Oh, my God, she's crazy, too."

"I think she got wetter than I knew," Oren said. Without

thought, he scrubbed at his thigh.

"Let's get to the garage and load up," Pax said. "Now. That girl yowling is going to attract more crazies." He watched Oren rubbing at the damp spot.

"Rainies," Oren whispered as he followed them to the kitchen.

"What about Rick?" Lydia asked. Once, the skinny man had gotten up the nerve to ask her out, but that was before she started dating Chris, and she had half-heartedly considered going out with him for about three seconds. He was a nice man, an honest person, but he was normally jittery and chatty; he would have made Lydia nervous on a date.

"Rick?" Oren called.

The man might have blinked in response, but he didn't look up. He had stopped drying himself but was still holding a pink, fluffy towel by his side as if he had forgotten what he had been doing. For all his nervous energy and constant chewing of antacids for his nervous stomach, the man had burned out. In a way it was interesting to look at him without the worry furrows on his face or the tight lines about his lips and his darting eyes. Calm, he looked like a different man, satisfied and almost handsome.

Lydia wondered what that felt like: to give up every fear and concern and be at peace. Rick didn't look unhappy; he was in a state of relaxation.

"Let's go," said Pax as he pulled Lydia's arm and got her moving again. Dana sat with Dan in the front; Pax, Annie, and Oren sat in the back seat, and Lydia, Sammy, and Dana folded themselves into the small space in the back. Dan waited until the garage door opened, and then he backed out in a straight line. When he was sure he was in the street, he turned the car to face south.

At the door, Mandy stopped banging for a second; she had been joined by two of the neighbors, and more of the neighbors sloshed in the water aimlessly, as smooth as Rick was. Mandy and the other two watched for a second and then began banging again.

Dan drove onto Hickory and then into the T intersection

where the van lay on its side and the police cruiser sat, crumpled. He gingerly skirted the wreck, looking out at the fields that were like lakes.

After a block, he turned left onto Main and drove to the Main Street Hotel. Ignoring the landscaping, Dan decided to use the area close to the doors.

He sighed as he turned off the engine.

The hotel was like an island in the storm. Literally.

Chapter 8

At the overhang, Mark jumped out of his cruiser and shed the hot, heavy slicker and trash bags, trying to cool off, and stop the infernal sweating that felt as if he were getting rain-soaked.

The front desk where patients checked in was empty as was the waiting room; that alone was kind of eerie since it was never totally empty. A streak of bright red blood was splashed on the side of the counter, and squishy wet, pink footprints were leading toward the door; no one was in sight. Some of the chairs in the waiting room, cheap plastic things in orange and blue, were turned over.

Mark shrugged. His gun was out, and Mitch and Sara followed behind him.

"What do you think? Emergency Room?" Mitch whispered. "You know in movies, you never want to go to the hospital because that's where the zombies came from. They start there."

"They aren't zombies," Sara whispered.

"Okay, they aren't, and what will you do if I stupidly suggest we separate and go look around the place alone?"

"Then, I'd kick you in the shin. Stop being an asshole."

Mark held back a chuckle, "Riiight. I'll try."

Mark quietly pushed through the Emergency Room doors. Gus lunged forwards with a big metal bar in his hands, his eyes very focused and alert. He wasn't 'messed' up by the rain, but because he was being protective of the people there, he knew it was best to know the difference.

Mark had time to notice the end of the bar was matted red with gore. "Gus, hey, it's me. I'm okay."

"Are you sure?"

"Yes, I'm sure. Are you...*you*?"

"Who in the hell else would I be, Mark?" Gus asked, flummoxed.

"We came to get all of you and take you to the Main Street Hotel. It's the highest point, and we can hole up together until the military comes to rescue us. Coral and Oren said to go there."

"I thought you were another one of the Rainies. I done had to beat down two of them. One was Jerry Cash."

"No shit? Jerry?" Mark said.

"He came in all wet and mad and was waving a baseball bat. I crept up and pow, he's down for the count."

"Did you kill him?"

"Hell, I don't know. I popped him, tied him, and dragged him into a room. Do you wanna go check and then play some cards and hey, you two can have a beer…." Gus shook his head. "I took him out. If you can do better, then please do so."

"Just give me an sitrep."

Gus tilted his head, "You want a what?"

"Just tell me what all of you have going here or about the situation. I need a report on the situation, Gus. Who is here?"

Gus explained that one of the orderlies was there and was okay, and so were a doctor, two nurses, and a handful of patients, but everyone else they had seen was a *Rainie.* The little hospital had been almost empty of patients. {Gus knew what a sitrep was because he watched movies and read, but he enjoyed giving Mark a rough time}.

Mark told him, "We need to grab some supplies and get out. If the crazies…Rainies…whatever they are come here and cut us off from the Winnebago, then, we are up a creek. Ummm, literally. Mitch, I want you and Sara to go back to the 'Bago and be ready, okay? Send those other two guys my way."

Mitch and Sara went out and climbed back into their motor home and asked the two men who waited to go inside and see Mark. Sara shivered and found a sweater. "That was creepy in there."

"It was spooky; it's a good thing that guy, Gus, is there to help Mark."

Marnie walked over, glad to see the officer. She said that the man they had brought in, the one with the deep slashes to his belly, had died. His wife refused to leave his side. "We did all we could, but he was really messed up."

"Sorry, we'll get the rest."

Dr. Roberts glared at Mark. "I can't believe you expect to

move my patients. We have the generator going. You won't have electricity at the Hotel. These people need care, and we can give them that here. No one is going with you."

"I understand that, but Dr. Roberts, if...no...*when* you get another Rainie in here attacking with a gun or knife or a *fork*, what do you plan to do, then?"

"I expect you to be here to protect us until we get rescued."

"I put down two," Gus reminded them. {He had gotten two, and Mark had gotten one, so Gus was ahead}.

"We'll lock the doors, and Rodney is here." The doctor motioned to the big orderly.

"No...un-huh...Rodney ain't anywhere here," the younger man said. He was well built and strong as an ox, but he wasn't about to fight with crazy, wet people. He shook his head and went back to packing supplies.

"I'll fire you."

Rodney shrugged, "'kay."

"So get away from all my supplies. Get out of the hospital. You are fired."

Rodney looked at Mark, whom he had gone to school with and hung around with since. The doc had just met his match in Mark. Rodney opened up a cabinet and took out what he thought might be needed.

"What are you doing with that? Those are medications that are kept locked up," Dr. Roberts roared. He looked at Mark as if he wanted Mark to arrest the orderly.

"Maybe so, but we need medical supplies, Doctor, and if you won't come and help, then we'll take what we need. Consider that the city of Cold Springs, led by Chief of Police, Oren Hastings, is confiscating that stuff," Mark snapped back.

"I intend to file a complaint."

"You do that."

Rodney nodded and went back to packing. Marnie skittered off to pack a bag of supplies, as well. They loaded bandages and suture kits, vials and syringes, tape, gauze, and scissors, medications: pain, antibiotics, antiseptics, bags of glucose and saline solution, Novocain, a stethoscope, IV tubing, and anything else medical.

"You are going to kill these people if you move them," Dr. Roberts said. He followed Mark to each room, giving his opinion and reminding him they had the generator and food and that he was staying there in the hospital. The elderly wife of the dead man refused to look at Mark and didn't listen to either side, but her body language made it clear she was staying where she was.

In the next cubical was a girl who had been cut badly by Chris. Her arms and neck were bandaged and taped thickly, and she was asleep, with her boyfriend next to her. "He gave her something for the pain. I don't know how we could get her moved.... This has to be over soon, and the National Guard will come help us."

"That's right," Dr. Roberts said.

"It's not just here. The State Boys said this is there, too."

The boyfriend of the young women shook his head tiredly. He wasn't going either. Dejected, Mark gave up another two to the doctor.

The girl who had fought crazy Daisy was in the next little room with her mother. Her name was Carrie. Mark thought she was in high school and maybe a cheerleader. "How's the arm?"

Carrie sighed, "Hurts some, not too bad."

Mark and the doctor both gave their spiels.

Carrie narrowed her eyes. "Officer, did you see Daisy when my dad was done? He kicked her head in." Her voice caught, and she cleared her throat, sipping at water her mother offered her.

"I think Dad got rain on himself from Daisy, and he attacked her. He saved my bacon for sure, but he went nuts on her. We came here, and I got patched up." She held up her arm. She received a shot of antibiotics and an IV with saline and antibiotics, had her wound scrubbed out well, was stitched and bandaged with thick, soft gauze, had a few shots of Novocain, and was taped and wrapped fully.

"I'm sorry."

"My dad just got partially wet. He held himself together other than kicking Daisy to death. But we came here, and he struggled. You could see it in his eyes. He was torn between that anger and violence and being my dad," said Carrie as she glanced at her mother, Susie, who was crying softly. "All of a sudden, *it* was too much, and he was grabbing at his head and saying it itched and hurt, but he didn't hurt us. He gritted his teeth, and he ran, and I mean *ran* out of here; I guess into the rain to finish whatever *it* does."

"I'm sorry," Mark said again.

Carrie nodded. "I don't know what he did once he was that way. Maybe he is still pissed off, or maybe he's like a zombie without emotions, but I don't want him breaking in here. I don't want to see that. So we're going with you," she said as she motioned to a nurse that hovered. "Please unhook me. I am leaving."

"You need an antibiotic drip. You're going to get an infection…."

"Unhook me."

Dr. Roberts advised her not to go, but Carrie waved him away; she and her mother prepared to leave. One of the men with Mark decided he would stay, making Dr. Roberts grin with another win for his side. One of the nurses, Tina, said she was going with Mark, and he grinned right back at the doctor.

Mark had Rodney, Tina, Susie, Carrie, David, Marnie, and Gus with him. The other patients: a heart patient, a dehydrated drunk tourist, and the little girl with the broken arm, and her parents wouldn't go.

At the last minute, a man named Jack who had cut himself with an axe and who was new to town decided he would go.

"Win some, lose some," Dr. Roberts quipped. "Mark, you alone are responsible for what happens to these people because they need to be here to have proper care. Just keep that fact in your head."

"If these people are attacked and hurt, it's on you," Mark hissed. He was aware that Oren or Ronnie would have forced all of them to go with some double talk and threats, but Mark wasn't sure how to go about that.

"We are going to go out, slowly and steady. We have to go through the waiting room and out the doors. The RV is right there under the portico, so it will be nice and dry."

Mark and Gus went first.

As Marnie came through the doors, she made a scared noise that sounded like a mouse caught in a trap.

In the waiting room, five people stood. They had been trying to get out of town and thought the hospital was a good place to gather; however, the car that they were in skidded on the wet pavement and crashed into the Doughnut and Sweets Shop across the parking lot from the hospital.

The driver quickly was soaked by the rain, which pelted through the hole in the windshield that his head had made. He was trapped in the wreckage, almost crushed.

The teen {in the *sports car-go crash* } beat at the steering wheel, gnashing his teeth at the others and struggling to get free to rip them to pieces. Unmindful of his broken bones and deep cuts, he fought the rubble to get free. In a panic, the passenger on his right and the three in the backseat grabbed umbrellas and pulled their hoodies over their heads and ran for the hospital.

In shorts and flip flops, jeans and sneakers, they were soaked by the time they reached the doors to the hospital but barreled inside anyway.

Mark and Gus stared at the five teens.

The teens shook their heads, growled, and felt a rising fury towards the people they saw. Had they stayed in their apartments, they would have been fine. Had they stayed on 3rd Street, they might have been okay, but now they were wet, and the *'frog was in the bugle'*, compelling them to rip apart everyone they saw before they went smooth.

Mark leveled his gun and said, "You wanna stay back."

One of the boys, hands cramped into claws, ran at Mark and Gus. It was his intention to tear each finger off of the people he saw, then the hands, then all of the arms. Mark released his breath and fired; three of his four shots hit the boy in the chest area.

Two girls rushed them.

Mark used his last two shots and dropped one of them.

"Oh, boy," Gus called out. Mark was already fumbling with

his speed loader, but the loading of his gun was anything but speedy.

Gus first poked at the girl, knocking her backwards. She was tall with long, coltish legs, had a Romanesque face with strong features and long, glossy blonde hair that swept her shoulders like corn silk. The rain had dampened the silk, molding it to her head. Had she not been in this situation, she would have been a pretty woman, and a beautiful senior with her classic features. Gus didn't think all of this, but he did appreciate her attractiveness.

While he tried to maneuver her into a spot where he could bash her head, the other two attacked: a boy and girl.

Marnie, Carrie, and Susie ducked to the side; both women tried to protect Carrie and her injured arm. Rodney, the orderly, yanked the nurse Tina to the corner and pulled a wheelchair in front of them. He grabbed a chair and jabbed its legs toward the attackers.

David, the man who had come with Mark in the RV, grabbed a clip board and began to fight with the girl, leaving Jack to fight with the boy: he tackled him.

Earlier, Jack had been cutting down a tree in his yard and had hit his leg instead. Luckily, it was just a bit more than a long nick that had needed a few stitches.

Gus now had the girl where he wanted. He slammed the pipe down on her head at an angle as if he were knocking out a home run.

Her sturdy body went poker-stiff, and she dropped to her knees with a terrible thud. Wincing at her ruined kneecaps, Gus slammed the pipe home once more; the girl dropped to the ground and didn't move again.

On the floor, Jack and the boy were having a fistfight. The boy ripped Jack's stitches loose and dug into the axe wound, raked open furrows down Jack's cheek, and almost had squeezed the man's testicles off.

Jack had managed an uppercut to the boy's jaw that hardly affected him. As Jack hugged himself into a ball, cradling his damaged manhood, the boy grabbed Jack's head and slammed it into the hard floor.

Jack's head now hurt as much as his testicles ached, and he struggled to crawl away from the assault.

The girl who fought David had bitten his arm twice and taken a chunk out of his shoulder with her teeth. Her dark hair whipped about, making her look like a possessed witch; she snapped her jaws at David and kicked at his legs, trying to roll on top of him and get another bite.

He clasped her throat in his hands and struggled to raise her off of him. But in seconds, he would tire as she squirmed snake-like, and she would fall on his throat and rip it out. He knew this.

"Zombie bitch," Mark yelled. He fired three times, and one of the shots hit the girl in the back, knocking her off of David. He didn't look as David scrambled to his feet and hefted a table made of faux wood. He didn't look when he heard the terrible cracking sound and thud. He didn't look as the sound repeated.

Gus hit the boy who sat on Jack's chest, digging at his neck. Blood covered Jack's leg; the bandage was torn away, and the axe wound was wide open. His neck had been worried and dug at until it also opened up. The boy yanked at the flesh, tearing it opened wider, ignoring the slippery blood pooling. When Gus hit him, the boy slid off of Jack, his arm broken by the pipe.

As the boy raised the other arm and lunged at Gus, Mark shot him.

The silence was heavy.

Chapter 9

Curiously, Marnie and Rodney ran over to look at the boy. "He's alive. See his chest? It's a sucking wound. You can hold it shut, " Marnie said, "Dr. Roberts might can do something."

"Do you wanna give him first aid?" Mark asked her.

"No." She went to where Rodney knelt by Jack. Blood was everywhere; Jack's carotid artery had been torn open, and he had bled out. Rodney shook his head in defeat.

"She wasn't really a zombie, was she?" David asked Mark.

"I dunno what she...they are. No, she's not a zombie."

David let out a heavy breath. "I have been bitten. If she's a zombie, I'll turn, too."

"She isn't no zombie," Gus said. "I don't think she is anyway. Do you feel...you know...like you want to bite and eat someone?"

Tina had run back into the Emergency Room to grab additional supplies, ignored Dr. Roberts' snide remarks and taunts, and then ran back with what she needed. Telling the rest she needed a second, she bathed David's bite with antiseptic which set him to cursing loudly, then packed one wound with gauze, and bandaged and securely taped the rest. She gave him a painful shot of antibiotics.

"Why are you doing that? I'm gonna turn."

"Turn into what?" Tina asked him. She gave him something for the pain.

Mark looked at the girl that David had finished with on the table, her head a leaking, mashed thing. "He thinks he's gonna turn into a zombie and bite and eat people. He thinks the girl was a zombie."

"I think you'll be fine, but if you feel *zombieish*, you tell me right away, and I'll pop you in the head so that you don't turn. Deal?" Gus asked, "I have your back."

David cast him a withering look.

Mark told them it was time to get out before they were attacked again.

Outside under the cover, they were dry and were able to go right to the RV where Sara helped Carrie, Susie, and Tina into the vehicle. When everyone was inside, Sara and Mitch looked at Mark expectantly. "We saw those crazies, and we heard the gun shots."

"We took care of them. We lost one guy who was with us. And David is bitten and thinks he is gonna become a zombie."

"I can't believe these are all the people who would come with us," said Mitch while starting the RV. He pulled out, and they heard the tapping: Pitter-patter of rain on the top of the RV. The sky was lightening with sunrise.

"Look," Sara said. Mitch slowed down and came to a stop as he came to 2nd Street. "What do you think?"

Mark came forward to look at Mitch's shoulder. A half dozen people stood in the intersection, looking at the Winnebago, deciding if they would attack it or keep going.

The people in the RV had never seen such hatred and fury on anyone's face. Each of the six in the rain looked as if he wanted nothing more than to rip and tear people apart and to cause as much pain and fear as possible.

In that moment, Mark had a revelation. That night that he had clubbed a man unconscious with his sidearm, he had shot and killed three people, and he had watched people die. He had been on the force ten years and had wanted to be a cop since he was a kid. He had found it to be a good vocation, quiet mostly, and he always had self-pride that he was fairly good at his job.

But he had been skimming along. In a bigger town or city, he would have worked much harder and faced much worse. Anywhere else, he would have dealt already with the incidents that he had faced one rainy night.

Mark would see this through and do as well as he could, but the plain truth was that tonight he had been most unsure of himself, more afraid, and more horrified than he could ever have imagined in his worst nightmares. He didn't want to get wet and hurt anyone and *go smooth,* but he understood if someone did want to, as terrible as this was, it was much easier than being scared shitless every second.

Being one of them had to be better than being so damned afraid.

"Run over them," Sara whispered. The thought both terrified her and seemed right; she was just scared of the people in the rain. *Rainies.*

"I could," Mitch whispered back.

'*Do it.* Do it,' thought Mark. Do it like David had done it by bashing in the girl's skull with a table until her brains leaked out. Do it like he had done when he shot those crazies. Run them over. He wasn't angry like they were. He was afraid. 'So, *do it.*'

"Go around them," Mark said. The moment was gone.

Mitch maneuvered the big vehicle to the left and turning, and then at the Catholic Church across from Coral's Diner where all of this had all started, he turned left again and pulled into the hotel's portico.

The half dozen angry people watched the big RV drive away and then returned their interest to the hospital, which was brightly lit even against the sunrise. They walked to the building.

In a few minutes, screams filled the morning as the six tore the people to shreds who were still in the hospital. When they finished, they walked around a while, unsure of what to do next.

In an hour, they stopped walking and stood in one place, faces as blank as statues of marble. In an hour and a half, they were unable to respond to anything around them.

They had gone *smooth.*

Chapter 10

Coral drove carefully.

He went all the way down 2nd Street and turned left on Elm. He saw the laundry mat, police station, and fire station on his left and the library and school on his right. At the intersection of Elm and 1st was the courthouse on the corner. He stopped there.

"What do you think?" he asked Katie and Jobie.

"I think the water is pretty deep. And it's dark," Jobie said. He wanted to go check on his parents, but Coral said they had to come here first. With the headlights and spotlights beaming from Coral's big Ford Explorer, they could see the dark water as it flowed south. A lot of trash was in the water: plastic and paper and leaves and branches swirled and twisted as they bounced off the stones of the school and kept going. A large tree turned over in a heavy sweeping motion that drove trash around it.

But before he could hit the brakes, the Explorer slipped down 1st street towards the lake. Once in a while, there was a lump of clothing and pale limbs that could only be human. {Although the two who watched might pretend those were bleached tree branches}.

"I think there are people in the hotel, and they can see us but can't come down because of the water," Jobie said. "Mr. Coral, they may be up there, wondering why we can't help them and what they're gonna do. I bet they're scared."

"I guess we're all scared."

Katie whined. Coral patted her head absently.

"There's nothing we can do," Jobie said.

Avoiding the deeper water, Coral backed up until he was in front of the police station. Ronnie pulled her cruiser into one of the car bays, and Coral pulled into the other.

After Ronnie unlocked the weapons cabinet, she and the rest loaded up the Explorer with extra ammunition, a pair of Glock .22s, and three Remington .870s. She added a stack of rain gear, some flares, a few sets of handcuffs, and several flashlights.

Ronnie tried to reach the State Police on the radio but got no response. She tried other bands, but no one was there. "How can they all be gone? Someone should answer."

"Maybe they're busy, " Coral said, "you've been busy." He told Ronnie that they hadn't seen anyone on the street but that they felt people were in the hotel, not knowing what to do or how to keep from being frightened.

"Besides a boat...a boat with a cover on top, how would anyone get out of there anyway?" Jobie mused. "We've all been getting damp, so I think it takes a substantial amount of rain directly on the skin to make someone sick, but you'd still need a really dry boat to be safe."

He shrugged and said he didn't have any more ideas as he climbed into the cruiser with Ronnie. She gave Coral, Jake, and George a wave, promising to meet them at the hotel as soon as they got Jobie's parents and sisters safely into the cruiser.

Chapter 11

"Jobie, you've been very brave tonight. I know your parents will be super proud of you."

"Thanks, Miss Ronnie. Mostly all I've done is watch. What do you think it feels like? I think it would feel like all the anger in the world, and maybe when you feel it, you want to destroy anyone who isn't angry. You'd want to rip him to shreds because you'd be changing and knew it. Then, I think everything inside, who you are, the personality part, just burns up and vanishes."

"Do you think people can come back? The personality part?"

Jobie frowned and answered, "I wish they could, but no, I think they're gone forever. Once something is burned away, it can't somehow regenerate."

"What do you think is causing it?"

"It could be anything, right? Maybe someone did it maliciously, but I bet it's natural: I like biology and other sciences, and I think Nature is a pretty tough b...ummm witch."

Ronnie snickered. She saw a deep puddle almost too late, slammed on the brakes and swerved. Instantly, she regretted not having Gus fix her car seat as it failed to hold, and she slid into the dashboard. She threw her left knee up to keep herself from plowing head first into the dash and breaking her ribs and collar bones, cursing that she had known better than to let this happen.

A bright light filled her head as enormous pain lit up her knee, radiating into her lower leg and into her hip. Her kneecap dislocated, sliding to the left as it took her full weight, ligaments tore, and Ronnie groaned loudly, ending with a small scream.

"Ronnie?"

She let Jobie worry and call her name without responding because she felt as if someone had hit her in the stomach and knocked her breath out. She had to concentrate just to inhale.

Black and white lights danced in her vision as she tried not to pass out. Finally, after several minutes, the pain was just bad enough to make her wish she could pass out; then, she was able to notice the cold sweat that had covered her and how hard she was gritting her teeth.

"I'm okay. Yep. I have it."

"Ronnie, you are really pale."

"I bet I am." She took a deep, slow breath and found that helped with her pain. She dug pain relievers out of her glove box and swallowed them dry. "Okay, we're going again slow...very slow, you ready?"

"Ready."

A block down, Ronnie turned left onto 3rd and then right onto Oak. She told Jobie to take his feet off of the floorboard since water was creeping up and the floor of the cruiser was beginning to squish with rainwater seeping in.

Although the car hardly crawled now, Ronnie worried that she was going to stall out. As she made the turn onto South Oak, waves pulsed outward to race across submerged yards.

"Look," Jobie pointed out a black SOS written on a pale blue bed sheet and hung from a window of the fourth floor apartments on their left.

In the hazy morning, it could barely be seen. "Why hasn't someone come to get us? Why hasn't the army or something come yet, Ronnie?"

"Maybe it's taking them a while or they're being careful not to get wet. And the bridge is washed out, so maybe that...."

"Or because it's happening over the bridge, too. Why would the poisonous clouds just sit above Cold Springs and nowhere else? That's impossible, isn't it? For clouds to do that? I know it is. I like science," Jobie said.

"Yeah, you mentioned that. What were you doing in the diner alone tonight without your family? Were you with friends?" Ronnie waited for the waves of water that she had caused to end.

"No, I was drinking a Coke and watching people. I like to do that, too. Last semester we had psychology, and that's a type of...."

"Science. And I bet you liked it. Behavioral science."

"Yes, and I didn't have anything else to do anyway. I don't have a lot of friends; they don't like things I like so much."

Like science, Ronnie thought.

"Stop," Jobie shouted and motioned to the side.

Ronnie stopped again and looked around the boy. From a small house, a man, woman, and child ran out onto their porch, pointing at the cruiser and shouting. Ronnie wondered how she could safely let them know they should go back inside where it was dry and wait and why they couldn't help them right now while it was pouring rain.

Ronnie took the time to feel sorry for herself and silently cursed the pain of her left leg. It was almost over-taking her. She understood how the crazies were consumed by anger; she was almost consumed with the pain in her poor knee.

Jobie made motions to the family, indicating they should go inside and wait. "They don't know sign language," he said.

"Should they?"

"It would be easier to tell them to wait inside if they did," Jobie answered, "I know it."

" Most don't know it. Plan B is to make them understand. Pantomime," Ronnie said, "Jobie, what the hell?"

She screamed.

To the right, a door flew open, and a man in blue jeans and a tee shirt came out; in one hand, he held a can of beer, and he was followed by a woman with short hair in a faded, saggy sundress and a little boy in a diaper and little ball cap. The woman and toddler were a few steps behind the man. The baby had a ratty stuffed animal in one hand.

A pit bull ran past the woman who lunged for his collar, jumped into the water, and swam toward the car.

In a second, he turned back the way he had come and swam back to the porch where the woman waited for him, calling his name. Back on the porch, once he had crawled and scratched back to the dry boards, he ran to one side and shook off the dirty water. Then, he began barking at Ronnie and Jobie in the car.

The man was waving his hands energetically, almost frantically and kept coming; the water was almost to the porch's floorboards, but he didn't pause. The man stepped off of his porch and didn't land on the top step but slid down the steps as he misjudged and landed in the water, cracking his back, butt, and shoulders on the stone steps and smacking the back of his head on the porch.

"I motioned him to go back," Jobie yelped.

The man splashed a few seconds but could do little more than get his eyes and nose above the water. Instead of slinking below the surface, he barred his teeth and pulled his way to his feet, gripping the handrail tightly.

Behind him, his wife and child made noises of concern and fear, and the man's head whipped around to locate them.

The dog shook off again, catching them in his droplets of spray. Their eyes went wide. As the mother's face began to take on the familiar fury, the toddler plopped down on the porch and started to wail and wave his fists.

Jobie snapped his head around to stare straight ahead, holding one hand to the side of his head and eye to keep from peripherally seeing what the man and his family were doing. He didn't want to see that man hurt the woman or child.

Ronnie drove forward so that they couldn't see what was happening. If she could have stayed dry by leaning out the window, she might have tried to shoot the man to save his family, but Ronnie didn't know of a way to stay dry, and she doubted she could make the shot anyway. The dog had gotten them wet anyway, to some extent.

She stopped the car. Despite her tough exterior, Ronnie began to cry. In a second, she was bawling her head off, heaving and wiping snot off her nose, just making a mess of herself. She felt Jobie reach over and pat her hand and then keep his hand close. Her knee hurt, and the man was going to rip into his family, and it was raining poison. She was having her damned period, which always made her feel weepy and crampy, and her job right then, just sucked.

She squeezed his hand and held on tightly.

To Jobie's credit, he didn't laugh at her or say anything meant to be soothing but gripped her hand tightly while she cried.

When she was finally empty and finished, Ronnie wiped her face and blew her nose a few times. She dug two bottles of water out of the glove box, handed one to Jobie and drank one herself.

Jobie handed her a piece of minty gum, which she

unwrapped and popped into her mouth.

"Jobie, for the record, those kids aren't your friends; they are a bunch of dumbasses. They are just idiots...full of bullshit...really stupid kids. They are missing out on having a good, real friend," Ronnie told him passionately.

Jobie chuckled, "You cursed."

"I did." She smiled a little.

{The pain in her knee was the worst pain she had ever felt}.

She drove down towards the end of the street where his house was. The yards were even lower down there, closer to the swampy area off the lake and were deeply submerged. Dirty water swirled over the porches ahead, running into the homes. All were wooden one-story houses, and everything inside would be ruined in each of them. People caught at home would either be standing on furniture out of the water or turned crazy {Rainie} {Smooth} by now.

Ronnie stopped snickering at Jobie and felt like crying again.

"My sisters don't know how to swim," Jobie said conversationally. "They are supposed to learn, but the lake is closed, so Mom and Dad said 'wait 'til this year, and they could learn.' What do you think happened to them and all the other people on my street?"

"I dunno. I guess some will be okay because you know things are that way. There are always miracles in times like this. You hear about heroes and magical things later. I just don't know, Jobie."

"I think it's raining less. I can see better." Jobie watched out the window. He shuddered as a loud scrape ran from bumper to bumper beneath the cruiser, and Ronnie beat at the steering wheel with frustration when she tried a three-point turn.

Caught sideways in the street, the Crown Victoria shimmied to a stop.

"What's wrong?"

Ronnie turned the steering wheel different ways, tried the accelerator, and even rocked her body back and forth; the grinding noise still came from under the car, but they weren't moving. The undercarriage of the car was caught on something, and they weren't moving, regardless of what Ronnie tried. She broke out in a sweat as she slammed her body backwards and then side to side, jarring her knee. Tears ran down her face.

"I think we're stuck," Jobie said.

"Damnit. We can't be," Ronnie said, but she stopped rocking and throwing herself about, "How can I be this stupid?"

"You didn't mean to get stuck; it just happened. It's like anyone else, you can't stop what nature throws at you," said Jobie as he jumped when a series of thuds hit his side of the car.

"Ewww." He watched the three human bodies, plus a cat, two dogs, and a cow bob along, the animals and humans had bumped the side of the car, and all were bloated.

The dead were swept along towards the apartments out of sight, but for a long time, Ronnie watched where they went. Several inches of water covered the floor of the cruiser, and when she moved her boots, the water splashed. "Jobie, it's getting deeper."

"My feet are up."

"I know. I don't mean...the water is still rising is what I'm saying. Just in a minute or two, it has risen a few inches in here. Look at the houses."

Behind them, water flowed over the porches and was covering some of the lower windows. It was more than halfway up the doors and sides. Closer to them where water had lapped at the porches, it was now streaming over and into the homes.

Where the family had stood was awash with filthy water and trash. Maybe the father had gotten to his wife and child, but if he hadn't, the water would now.

Jobie whirled around as a big dog slammed into his door before floating away on the current. This thud had been significantly higher on the door than the other ones. "What are we going to do?"

"I was thinking about that. We need to act fast before it gets too deep. You are going to have to roll down your window after you get into my slicker and the baggies, use the umbrella and that tarp to crawl out onto the ledge of the car window, and climb to the top.

Once you're there, you are going to have to sit tightly, stay still and dry under the tarp, and wait. Coral and the others will wonder what's taking us this long and come looking."

"Are you sure?"

"Positive. So you just sit there all dry and patient, and they'll come."

"You mean *we* will, Ronnie."

Ronnie shook her head, "I've been thinking hard, Jobie, and the thing is I have one sicker and enough baggies for really one person. The tarp will cover one person. Look over here; crawl on me if you have to...see my knee?"

Jobie stretched to look where she pointed. On the front of her knee where a slight bump of a kneecap was supposed to be, was a huge lump on the side where her knee had shifted and the top was kind of flat. Her slacks were loose fitting, but the fabric was pulled tightly over her sausage-leg and seemed about to split. He had known she hurt her leg, but this was far worse than he could have imagined.

"Oh, Ronnie."

"Yep, pretty bad, huh?" She shrugged and said, "I won't be climbing at all. I'd fall even if I could support my weight; the pain would buckle me."

"I can help you," he offered. He was a skinny kid and would barely be athletic enough to climb up there himself.

"Get into my slicker and get going. We can't wait around, or it'll get too deep in here," Ronnie ordered him. Jobie didn't move. "Jobie, you...."

"I heard you, Ronnie," he said softly. He noted the water was rising even faster. "If I get up there and the water comes in and you get wet, what do you imagine will happen?"

She blinked. She hadn't considered that. He was right, however, and when she got wet, she would ignore her pain and get out and go after him. No one would rescue him before she attacked. "I'll give you my gun. You'll have to...."

"I'm not gonna kill you! I don't know how to shoot a gun, and if I could, I wouldn't shoot you. I'd freeze or panic. I know for a fact I can't, Ronnie."

Her brain spun, trying to find a way out of this. "Okay, then you go on out, and I'll do it myself. God knows I don't want to turn into one of those Rainies."

Jobie's jaw dropped and he answered, "You can't, or you'll go to hell. Suicide is a mortal sin."

{It figured she would be stuck here with a damned Catholic}.

"Jobie, I'm running out of plans here. Can you just work with me a little?"

"I'm not leaving you. Please don't argue this with me because I don't want to be fighting as the water comes up. I can't leave you, and seriously, I'm a scrawny kid, so I can't do chin-ups or sit-ups in PE class.

I can't climb the rope or hit the volleyball when it comes at me. It usually hits me in the head, and Coach yells at me. The idea of my managing to pull myself to the roof and keep dry...." he chuckled softly and said, "is really amusing."

Ronnie put her head back, holding back another crying fit. "If I shot myself, then you'd have to...."

"Sit right here alone. Seriously. Do you think that's right? To leave me alone?"

"Are you scared?" Ronnie knew the water was about to pout into her boots now. It was almost up to their seats.

"No, yeah, kind of. It's not bad like drowning would be. Maybe we won't suffer; we'll just change and really won't know it."

"I'm scared to death," she said as she held his hand tightly. The water in her boot was warm, caressing her flesh, tingling. It didn't feel bad at all. Her legs relaxed, and the pain abated, slinking away to a far corner of her brain as she wiggled her toes in her wet socks.

"Ahhh," Jobie released a breath he was holding.

Thirty minutes later as the dark water covered the Crown Victoria's lights, neither Jobie nor Ronnie were alive but had drown calmly, without fighting the water. The anger had emerged for only a few seconds, but no one dry was around to attack, and they both welcomed the peace and nothingness that enveloped them like warm blankets.

A new lake was forming from the river and rain water, and the police cruiser sat at the bottom of the new lake, two bodies inside that still held hands tightly; both their faces were free of expression, calm, and very *smo*oth.

Part Three

Chapter 1

When Coral saw that Ronnie, Jobie, and his family hadn't gone to the hotel yet, he told George and Jake to get out, and he and Katie went to take a look. He could handle Oak, but he couldn't get to the turn-off to go down South Oak at the apartment buildings because the water was too high on his big Explorer.

Using binoculars, he looked at the last houses on the street; they were covered to their windows and were half way under the water. The way the street dipped, Coral figured that by the middle of the road, the houses would be submerged, and at the end, where Jobie's home was, the houses would be covered by many feet of water.

Coral didn't see the police cruiser on the street and knew the officers couldn't be on the far side on Farm Road because it was under water. They weren't to the east because that direction was flooded out. Only a small area was where the car could be, and yet, it wasn't there.

"Katie, I think they had some trouble. I don't think we're going to find them on dry land."

Katie whined in agreement.

One spot kept getting his attention. He didn't know what he was seeing until he imagined the cruiser sideways and not straight on. Coral realized he was seeing the very tops of the lights in the dirty water as it swirled.

Coral felt it in his gut: Ronnie and Jobie were gone.

He drove around carefully, going slowly. Coral went to the hotel to meet with the rest, driving into the circle drive under the portico where the others had parked.

Pax met Coral at the doorway with a warm handshake.

He told him about their adventures, all that Oren had been through, and about the hospital, and said that Oren had not really taken charge but mostly everyone was asking *him* what to do, so he was glad Coral was there to take over. Pax knelt and gave Katie hugs and kisses, scratching at her ears and rubbing noses with her.

"Why me? I'm not a leader."

"Sure you are, Boss," Pax said.

"Jeez, I'm really not."

"We think you are a very good leader."

"I have some guns in the Explorer and ammo that we should take out and secure. I don't want everyone to know where the stuff is or have the guns. Only Oren and Gus, Mark, Dan, Jake, George, and you, and Annie, that's who I trust."

"Appreciate that, Boss."

"I trusted Ronnie and the kid, Jobie. Level heads."

Pax paused a second and looked up. He had known Coral for less than twenty-four hours yet he was trusted; it meant a lot. "Okay, Katie. Go find Annie."

Following the big former football player, Pax wrapped the guns back in a blanket to take into the building. He wasn't an expert with a weapon, but Pax felt okay about carrying one and knew he was competent. He got the feeling something more than the obvious was bothering Coral.

"What do you want?" Coral motioned to the guns.

"Glock is fine," Pax said. "What's bothering you? Where are Ronnie and Jobie?"

"I don't know. I think the car is underwater down at the middle of the street close to Jobie's house. I'm not positive, but it looks as if that's what it is, and that's where they went. The whole neighborhood is flooded, and some of the places...you can barely see the roofs down south, but that cruiser isn't on any other street, not any of the streets I could get to that aren't under water."

"So you're saying they just kind of vanished?"

"I'm saying something happened, and I think they're in the water. I'm pretty sure they're gone. I dread telling Oren. I'm trying to get it right in my head before I tell him."

"Okay. I'll show you what we have going," Pax said as he pointed everything out to Coral as Dan and Jake came to get some of the weapons.

Marnie and Tina had a medical area set up in one of the conference rooms, and supplies filled the kitchen area of the hotel. Usually the hotel offered a small buffet breakfast for people to sit and eat in the quaint, roomy dining room.

"They were about a quarter full, and of those people, more than three-quarters were out and either never returned or came back pissed off and were locked out. What we have left is about a dozen people who were staying here and two employees, don't recall their names."

"Just two?"

"Two others went out to get something they needed and never came back."

"Where are they? Where are all the Rainies? We've seen some, but not the masses we should be seeing," Dan said.

"They're hiding and staying dry," Coral said, "I think they are. Not the Rainies, but the regular people like us. People aren't stupid. They probably figured out what was causing everyone to go crazy before we did. We were slow. "Where?"

"Anywhere there's food and bottled water or drinks and a place to sit, maybe at the theatre or spa. The museum has a snack bar. The barbeque place maybe. At the B and Bs."

They were gathering or in their homes, staying dry and quiet and waiting for someone to come along and save them or for the rain to stop and everything to dry. They would stay hidden until either they were rescued or the food and water ran out where they were.

"If they ran out, maybe, they'd run over here to get our food? Is that what you mean?" Dan asked. He told Coral what Sammy had heard: this was happening all over. "We can't let them come and take our food. It's ours."

"We'll protect it."

"They can bring their own food or whatever to add to our stash. They have to bring their own supplies and contribute," Dan continued, "and all people have to contribute. We need help."

Coral brought up the idea of not just locking the doors but blocking off the doors and windows and posting guards at the one door they would have available. "Can you set that up, Dan?

"On it, Coral. None of them will come to get our food. Uh-uh. No way. I'm on it, Coral," Dan said as he removed his ball cap, ran a hand through his hair, and replaced his hat.

"Pax, can you coordinate with Dan? Women and children can help this one, but I think we need someone on the top floor watching with the binoculars for anything such as Rainies or people coming over, a rescue team, or anything we need to know about. We need a look-out."

"Gotcha. How do you want to do food and water rations and who should do it?" Pax asked.

Coral thought and responded, "Dana and Lydia are tough enough for that. Tell them to ration and plan a menu, and let me know how long we can go. Maybe set up a guard for the kitchen if you think we need one. Mark may be best for that."

"Coral, the hotel guy wants to know if he should lock the booze away or let people have it or what?" Jake asked, "what are we gonna do with the booze?"

"Make a cocktail hour and hold the drinking to two drinks per customer so that we don't have drunks. And ask Marnie and Tina what they need for medical...something for pain relief or washing injuries...whatever, and get all that to them and find a place they can lock it up."

"Gotcha. On it."

Thanks, Jake."

"Hey, Boss, I'm getting a list of all who are here and the rooms each will be in so that we can keep up with and find whomever we need when we need them."

Annie rushed by with Katie and a black kitten trailing her. When Coral pointed to the animals, Annie chuckled, "We found Blackie, and she's taking a liking to Katie; they follow me everywhere...."

"Good. We need a list."

"Okay, I've got things to do," Pax said as he started to walk away.

Coral snagged his shirt. "Pax?"

"Yeah, Boss?"

"Why do all of you call me that? Why is everyone asking me what to do?" Coral asked quietly. "I have no idea what I'm doing here."

"Well, don't tell anyone that because we think you know

exactly what you're doing, and we trust you. Roll with it, Coral," Pax whispered back, "and I've got things to do, Boss," he called over a shoulder.

Chapter 2

Coral found Oren helping with the blocking off of the back doors. He had already begun before Dan approached him. Coral admired how the police chief had people helping and how well they had blocked off the windows and doors in the back. "Oren, why aren't you leading this raggedy group?"

"I can follow the law and arrest the bad guys, but I've never been a leader, Coral. You are what everyone needs right now. You give people hope."

"All of you have gone crazy. You're nutty."

"Maybe so."

"If you want to lead, then tell me to get out of your way, and I will, okay?"

"It's a deal," Oren said, "hey, I promised Ronnie we'd talk when she got back. Where is she?"

Coral shook his head and finally met Oren's eyes. "Down Jobie's street; it's flooded out over the roofs of the far houses. They got into some type of trouble, and the cruiser is under water."

"Did you see them?"

"If they got out, then I don't know where they went. The apartments are above water, but I don't think they would have left the car. Something I just feel in my gut. I'm sorry Oren, and maybe I'm wrong, but...."

Oren clenched his jaw and nodded. He stood for a second, staring into space and looking a little confused; his face had lost the pinched, tight look and had relaxed.

In a second, he turned back to Coral and studied his face. He looked as if he were trying to puzzle something out: the lines returned around his eyes and mouth, the crease between his eyes came back, and sadness came back to his face again. "Ronnie," he said finally.

"Oren? Are you all right?"

"Awe, Coral. That's part of why I can't lead anything. I got wet, just a little on my leg, but more and more I keep having times when I forget for a second what I'm doing, and I just zone out, as the kids would say. I guess one time I'll do it, and that'll be it for me," he said as he made a face like a naughty child.

"I'm sorry. I didn't know just a little bit of the water would do that."

"So it seems," Oren said, "I think it must be like what some people go through...oldtimers...altimer...."

"Alzheimer's."

"Yup."

Coral shivered. "Try to hang on, Oren. I may have been elected the leader when I wasn't paying attention, but I need your help."

"I'm glad Ronnie doesn't have to watch me do this. It isn't even bad, just relaxing a minute and forgetting and not even thinking; it's pretty good. Thinking, well, it hurts like hell, doesn't it?" He rubbed a hand through his hair and then wiped at his eyes.

"Sometimes it does at that."

"It about killed me when Darla died, but I had to raise Ronnie, and that kept me busy. A parent isn't supposed to outlive his child. That isn't the right way, and Coral, it hurts something fierce, as if there's something in my chest ripping its way out. That's grief."

"I'm sorry, Oren. That doesn't fix anything, but I sure am sorry."

"I know. To be honest, I kind of hope this thing...whatever it is...runs the course and burns out my brain."

"No, Oh, naw...."

"Yeah, I do hope it all burns away. It hurts too much. I'd rather be smooth. Coral, you lost your parents early and have been on your own a while. Losing Darla and now Ronnie, I'm just tired of hurting, and, Son, I have now seen the other side, and it's awfully nice. But for now, I better work on blocking this area."

"Oh, yeah, I guess," Coral said, "I'm sorry, Oren."

"It ain't you that done it. All this, I think it is nature cleaning itself up and eliminating the blight," said Oren as he winked, "we're the blight."

"I don't believe that. We're humans, we can love and dream, and that means nature shouldn't get rid of us."

"Bullshit, Coral. We are a blight." Oren lifted his shoulders a little. He looked tired and had hollows beneath his eyes. "I need to get this all fixed up to keep us safe."

"I know you're the best for this."

"Thanks, Coral." Oren went back to moving things and covering the back doors and windows so that no one could possibly get inside.

Had Coral watched Oren, he would have noticed that the man went blank for a minute or so every hour, and then, later it was about every fifty-five minutes and then every fifty minutes.

And if Coral had been watching, he would have seen that as it happened, Oren began to wait for it almost expectantly, and that it lasted a fraction longer each time. And he would have seen that after a while, Oren didn't just accept those moments of being smooth, but he craved them.

Coral wouldn't understand giving it all away.

Chapter 3

Pax rubbed at his itchy skin, had a bit of a fantasy about hot clothes, shaving cream, and a sharp razor, and rolled out of bed. He always felt a little damp, kind of cold, never clean, and sleep deprived, seldom deep or refreshing. He went to bed tired and awakened almost as tired.

They had been here for days.

And at least he went to sleep with and woke up with Annie, sometimes beside him, sometimes curled around his body to stay warm. Pax hadn't had a chance to take her to a movie or to dinner or to have a normal relationship with her. They were subjected to clinging to one another to stay warm and lying there together, listening to the rain patter.

He pulled at the pile of blankets, pulling them up on her, and Annie, on her stomach, lost in exhaustion, didn't stir. Brushing a strand of hair from her face, he watched her sleep, the frown lines on her face set even during slumber. This wasn't how he wanted life to be with her; Pax felt cheated of his happily-ever-after.

He didn't have to look out the window because he knew it would look much as it had the day before and the day before that because not once during the night had the pattering of rain stopped. It made his head ache to hear the constant droning and random rumbles of thunder; it disrupted his sleep, it grated on his nerves, and it never stopped.

Here on the fifth floor, there was nowhere else to go, and while they could have slept on the third or fourth floors without any problems, Annie said she couldn't sleep at all if she were that close to the floodwaters below; she wanted distance between herself and the water. The glass of the window wasn't far enough away from the water.

Pax couldn't bring himself to touch the glass with the water streaming on the other side. He raised his hand but didn't touch the glass.

"Just stop," he whispered.

To the north, Pax could see the ruined grocery store where

they might try to get food when they needed more, and at the other end of the block was Coral's diner.

Presumably the family that stayed behind still hid, and the bound prisoners died of thirst and hunger in Coral's storeroom although no one spoke of that little thing.

Coral said his diner might have a few feet of water in it by now and that those tied and cuffed people would have drowned. Pax shivered. They had left them to face whatever happened with their hands and feet bound.

To the east, Pax saw the tops of buildings, he should have been seeing the gas station and the other tall hotel, but there was nothing there but empty water. There were no buildings, no streets, no riverbanks, and certainly no stone bridge.

To the west was the park and baseball field and beyond that were a farm road, farm houses, and farm fields of food, but Pax saw nothing but water.

It was all gone.

And it still rained.

If he had been able to look north or had gone to another window to look out, he would have seen the same flood water there as well, dotted here and there with a wet roof and broken at times by big trees floating past, bloated pets, occasional cars, and the swollen carcasses of entire cow herds. Human bodies swept along with the current.

"Pax?"

"Try to sleep a little longer. It's early."

Annie turned on her side and clung to his pillow as she fell back asleep. Pax thought that maybe sleeping was an escape for her, but he didn't blame her for taking a way out. He would do the same if he were able. Katie looked at Pax and curled around her kitten, Blackie to go back to sleep.

Downstairs, Lydia and Dana were serving the last of the eggs and big mugs of hot coffee or glasses of orange juice. Dana pointed to a big plate of buttered toast and told Pax to help himself. "Did anyone sleep?"

Dana's eyes were glassy and smudged beneath with purple circles; she shook her head. Lydia said that she had a little but that

Sammy had been out cold. She was one of the few able to sleep, despite the constant noise of the rain. "She can sleep through about anything."

"Must be nice," Pax said.

"I know," Lydia agreed, "I watch her and wish I could be out cold once in a while." She laughed.

"How is everything else?"

Coral sighed, "We had a suicide, two went out a window, and I guess that's three suicides. One was the hotel manager and then the other two were tourists."

"Damn. They went out a window?"

"Yup. Knocked it out and jumped. They got angry and fought."

Pax stretched. They sat on chairs around tables from the rooms. "They lost hope, I guess. We have to keep the hope. This situation has to get better, right?"

"You'd think," Lydia said.

The first floor was underwater, and they had moved everything they could upstairs, but while they had their food and medical supplies, they wouldn't last forever. The survivors didn't have the kitchen now to cook meals, so they had to make small, controlled fires to cook. Boiling water was a lengthy, difficult, and dangerous process.

In the last four days, the lower floor had flooded, and the second floor was beginning to fill. The beautiful old hotel was ruined by the nasty water, which flooded in and filled with sewage, trash, carcasses, and mud. Fabrics and antiques fell apart.

"We'll have to move things up again," Coral said tiredly. Maybe we need to go ahead and take all of the stuff up to five, not that the water will come up that far. Someone should be here to rescue us soon, but we can take things up that far just to be on the safe side."

"Just stop," Dana snapped.

"What?" Coral asked.

"Coral, we've listened for days about how the rain has to stop, it can't keep raining, someone is gonna come get us, and this can't continue. Well, it's bullshit. You hear me? Coral, that is just bullshit."

"Dana...."

"Shut up, Lydia. You know it, too." Dana slammed the coffee carafe down on a table and stared for a second at the plate of toast. They had potatoes, a makeshift fire pit to cook in, and some pasta and vegetables in cans. She looked at a small can of oranges, picked it up, and threw it like a baseball at a wall. "It's all bullshit. It had been from the start. We should have been outside or gone outside and let it happen."

"You're talking crazy," Lydia said.

"We have done all of this to keep from getting messed up by the rain, and then you go and say that?" Pax huffed.

"Yeah, I'm saying we should have gone with it in the beginning, and then we wouldn't be here scared to death, worried about the rain, and wondering when someone will come save us."

"And? So?" Lydia prodded

"We'd be better off smooth," Dana said it quickly.

"Really? You really want to be like this?" asked Dan as he walked in, dragging Oren with him, by pulling at the older man's shirtsleeve.

Oren was fully blank; his face looked twenty years younger, as that of a child with no worries. If reminded, he would use the bathroom on his own and eat if food were set in front of him, using his hands but not utensils. He didn't speak or act on his own. "Oren, tell me who Ronnie is."

"Dunno."

"She's dead Oren. Your daughter is," Dan said it and wiped tears that streamed down his face.

"Okay."

"You remember being chief of police? Hanging out with us at Brody's bar? You remember your wife? No?"

"No."

"See? He's blank, Dana. He's nothing," Dan snapped.

"Ask Oren if he minds it." Dana was furious, not because of any rain on her, but because of the rain itself.

She faced the old man, "Do you mind, Oren? Is it that bad? Do you still mourn your wife and daughter? No? Do you worry and toss in the bed and cry and are you waiting to go mad or drown? No?" She spun. "He don't care, Dan, but guess what? I'm scared shitless."

"Everyone is afraid, Dana," Dan snapped. Gus and some of the others heard the shouting and came to listen and watch.

"Stop doing that shit to Oren," Pax demanded, sickened by the display.

"Shut up," Dane screamed at Dan, "Oren isn't afraid. Do you get it yet?"

"I get it," Coral said, "I get it all. I thought you were tough, but you're just a whiner, Dana. Stop screaming and raving."

"Oh, this is the '*motivate Dana*' speech when I realize how silly I am being, and I buck up? Sorry, it ain't happening, Coral. That was four days ago," she spat, "besides, I'm right anyway." She laughed.

George came in and frowned at Dana.

"If we're gonna move things, then we better move, now. Marnie says to tell you that the girl Carrie's arm is infected, and Marnie and Tina can't get seem to get it straight.

They said they don't think they have the right antibiotics. David's bites are infected, too. Rodney's cough has gone deeper; Tina says he has pneumonia," George announced. "Bad as things are, they're suffering. My chest is hurting. Etta said I should tell you that, too."

"And we'd not be suffering if we had gone into the rain that night and gone smooth," Dana said, making her point.

Pax ignored her and asked Coral what they should worry about moving.

"All the food. Medical supplies. Towels, blankets, everything," said Coral as he joined the rest to start hauling everything up the stairs to the top floor. He didn't feel like arguing anymore. Everyday the water was deeper, no one had come for them, and if Sammy were right about what she had learned on the Internet and television, then no one was coming. They needed the rain to stop.

It had to stop.

Chapter 4

Annie gave Pax a wave as she came out of their room. Blackie, in her arms, suddenly went poker-stiff, her hair standing on end as she hissed and scratched. Annie let her go, and she ran, with Katie back into the room, scooting under the bed. Katie whined and looked prepared to defend Blackie.

The scream peeled down the hall again. Coral ran head long down the hall with Pax with Dan right behind him. Gus and Mark trailed them. The door was locked, so Coral stepped back a few feet and barreled into it, knocking it open as easily as he had knocked members of the opposing football team off their feet.

A family of four was staying in this room. The woman stood in the center of the room, her hands up as if pleading to her husband. He was beside the bed, next to a little girl he had beaten with the leg of one of the chairs he had broken. Her head was little more than pulp, her bones broken. Bright red was pooled under her, covered her, and streaked the man's bare chest and boxer shorts.

It was impossible to miss the bloody teeth that had flown out of her mouth and landed on the old brownish carpet. Her little arms, twisted and snapped, were to each side of her as if she had been making a snow angel on the covers of the bed.

White globs of what looked like mashed potatoes were all over the room.

At the woman's feet was a small boy, hardly more than a baby, his bottle dropped beside his crushed skull. His mother slumped to the floor to gather her child into her arms, wailing.

"What the hell?" Coral demanded.

The man, his eyes lost in fury, actually growled as saliva dripped to his chest and as he brandished the leg of the chair for a threat. He didn't seem to recognize those who had run into the room, his wife, or the children. Beside Coral, Pax groaned, "He's gotten wet."

Before Coral and Pax could tackle the man, Gus fired a shot, dropping the man. A neat hole appeared in the man's chest as a bigger hole slammed out of his back. Gus, taking a few steps closer, shot once more into the man's head.

"We had it, Gus."

"You didn't have it without a gun out and his being shot," Gus argued.

"We weren't gonna shoot him, just...."

"Coral, you can't tie people up and store them every place we go."

"We can't just kill them, either."

Gus motioned to the little girl and said, "Tell her that."

Sara and her husband, Mitch, had gotten the woman and her baby out of the room. Annie came in with an update. "She says she was in the bathroom and left all three asleep in the bed."

"Look, " Coral stepped back, "we need to get out of here, out of the room."

"The body?" Pax asked, confused.

"Not our problem." Coral pushed them back with his body. "Look there."

They all followed his finger and stared at the ceiling. Pieces of the plaster had been soaked by the rain and were falling in sticky globs all over the room.

Large sections were missing from over head of where he had been sleeping, and drops of rain dripped down onto the pillow and side of the mattress. His portion was sodden.

"The ceiling? I can't believe this," Dan grumbled. "We need to check the halls and then the rooms we are using and the ones we intend to use."

"Don't you think the fourth floor is high enough?" someone asked.

"For today and maybe tomorrow, maybe not in a few days. Maybe not sooner." Coral sighed. He ushered them out, and they stayed in one place until the halls and then rooms had been checked. Three more rooms couldn't be used because the rain was leaking into the ceiling and beginning to drip.

When Pax finally took a break, he watched Lydia and Dana trying to stay busy counting supplies and organizing. Annie sat a warm soda in front of him. Gus met his eyes, and the man shook his head, looking defeated.

"The bottom, the top, it just keeps coming," Gus said.

"That's why I said it was ridiculous to keep struggling. We should have gone into the rain," Dana said under her breath,

Lydia slammed a hand against her friend's shoulder hard enough to knock Dana into a wall and demanded, "Knock that shit off. You see out there in the hall? That's my kid, and that's why we don't give up."

Pax watched Sammy, pale and tired-looking, toss a small red ball along the hall away from her. She giggled a little. Blackie and Katie chased the ball, and then Katie paused to let the kitten get ahead, swat the ball, and run back to Sammy. Katie then picked the ball up in her mouth and politely carried it back. Sammy muttered a 'thank you' and gave each animal a pat on the head.

"Your child almost tripped me with the ball," Jake complained to Lydia as he came in.

"Sammy, toss it the other way a while."

"It'll still be in the hallway," Jake said.

Lydia put a hand on each of her hips, and said, "I want her where I can see her." She had time to frown at Jake before she went back to giving Dana a dressing down.

"It isn't as funny to watch Blackie."

"She's funny, no matter which way you toss it. Sammy, do like I say."

Sammy let her voice crawl into what Lydia called a *'whine zone'*. "She doesn't go as fast and slide as much 'cause it isn't as sloped."

Pax and Gus chuckled.

Annie stopped glaring at her two friends and smiled at Lydia. "See? It doesn't work the same."

"Yup. It doesn't *slope* as much," said Jake as he managed a chuckle, too. "That's why," he stopped speaking.

Pax's jaw dropped, and he spun, following Dan at a dead run.

"Oh, my God." Annie got it a second later, scooped up Sammy and handed her to her mother, then grabbed Blackie and Katie. "Coral," she yelled.

Pax told the rest as soon as he took a good look that this

was serious.

"How serious?"

Pax looked at Coral, "The foundation is bad on this side, like the roof is. It's falling in, but it's also crumbling and collapsing. We may not have much longer."

Chapter 5

Rodney's chest felt as if a huge weight were crushing him. He wasn't coughing now, only lying in bed, his fever raging. His appetite had long since gone away, and he wanted to give up as his lungs drown from the fluid of the pneumonia. It was almost funny that he was drowning inside where it was dry.

Marnie and Tina said if they had the right medications, he would be fine. Of all things, he had survived the rain to die of a common illness, but he was dying slowly.

On the other side of him, the teen, Carrie, was in poorer shape. Her arm had swollen badly, and the flesh had split for the thick yellowish pus to soak the bandages on her arm. Unfortunately, the place where the fork tines had slammed into her arm and into the bone didn't fully drain.

Tina and Marnie had soaked her with alcohol and antibiotics and tried to swab the infection out, but it went deeper, and thin red lines radiated up her shoulder as fever racked her body. The infection smelled terrible.

Today, Tina said they would have to remove Carrie's arm. If they didn't, she would die. Carrie and her mother, Susie, cried a lot, and Carrie asked how she could stand the pain, but Tina didn't have an answer.

They had nothing for the pain, and nothing better than a few sharp knives and maybe cauterization with fire to stop the bleeding. With that, Tina didn't know if Carrie could stand the shock, so that pain might be for nothing.

On another cot, David rocked with his own pain as his bites turned rotten. The human mouth contains hundreds of kinds of bacteria, some which have never been properly identified or studied, much less killed.

The girl who had bitten him wasn't a zombie and didn't carry a new virus or infection, only the hundreds of the usual types of bacteria. The bites became very infected, and his body had so many places that were dangerous now that no amount of cutting or sawing, cleaning or taking antibiotics would save his life.

Marnie and Tina could do nothing for these three, but

Marnie did pray with them. She answered them honestly: they couldn't be saved, the pain and misery would increase, and the situation was hopeless for them.

Rodney asked Tina for soup, pleasing her that he might be rallying. He wasn't hungry but wanted time without her in the room. She was a good woman and would have argued. "Would you help me, Susie? Rodney asked.

Susie wiped her eyes; she constantly cried over Carrie. "Help you? Do what?"

"I'm going downstairs," he tried to smile as he told her.

"You can't...that's...." Her words failed. The floodwaters were above the third floor, rising to the fourth, seemingly to sneak up inches at a time as they clawed to reach everyone and everything above them. The waters reached upwards. Always upwards.

"That's peace," Rodney said. Gently, he helped David to stand, taking most of the other man's weight. David managed a slight eager smile. He just wanted to stop the pain.

Carrie steadied herself and reached out to her mother for help. "I can't stand anymore."

Susie started to argue but felt drained and warm, and a sense of peace crept over her. She slipped her arms around her daughter and helped her walk into the hall, the two men behind them. She knew the feelings were surrender.

Carrie giggled. Before her mother could ask why she was giggling, Carrie whispered, "It's funny, Mommy. We have to sneak away to be free from the pain, or Tina will try to heal us."

Rodney struggled to breathe, aching and exhausted. His vision wavered. He was about to slip to the floor and take David down with him. A strong hand came out of nowhere to grip Rodney's thin frame; he almost yelped but asked, "What are you doing, old man?"

"He's hurting, Rodney." George's wife Etta reached to help David down the hallway. "You know he's a heart patient. He's been having bad pains all tonight." She held a door open so that they could enter the emergency stairwell. With the extra help, all three patients managed to get down the stairs.

At the landing, they looked down at the water, using the flashlight Etta had brought. "Totally unprepared, no light."

"Don't need a light, Etta," George said, "you're a good woman."

"And you're a good man, George," she pointed, "just a few down to the water, and then, it's like a big ole bathtub, isn't it? Only in a stairwell."

"It doesn't look so dirty in here," Susie said, "I like how the light flickers on it."

David sat down on a step, his feet a mere inch out of the water. He wiggled dizzily, but Rodney sat next to him, wedging in tightly. Carrie was about to argue with her mother, but Susie sat down and pulled her teen daughter onto her lap as if she were a little girl. She hugged the girl and let Carrie bury her face in her neck as she cuddled.

"Don't waste your breath, old man," Etta warned George.

He slumped to sit next to the rest, unable to argue as pain rocketed through his heart, up and down his arm, in his chest and neck. He groaned with the misery.

"Father, hear our prayers," David whispered.

"Amen," Etta intoned as they pushed themselves forwards into the water.

Anger tickled their brains, confusion washed warmly over them, and peace settled in behind the other emotions as they chocked and gasped, slapping at the water a few seconds before letting it take away the pain and fear.

When the cries and splashing finally went silent and no more sounds echoed in the stairwell, a figure, a floor and a half above, sighed, her voice hitching as she sobbed, and tears ran down her cheeks.

Tina felt a terrible sadness fill her chest and throat, but she was finally able to walk the few steps upwards to the landing and open the door to the stairwell and go out.

With the door closed, she slid down and had a long cry for her patients.

Chapter 6

In the morning of the seventh day, Mark shot himself.

In the afternoon, the survivors looked out of the window as they always did, watching the water, wondering if someone were coming to get them. None of the other buildings were above the water now.

"What's that?" someone asked

"A cow."

"What's that?"

"Trash. Boards," were the answers to the question.

Over and over someone would spy something and ask what it was, hoping, making believe he was waiting for something. The rest would say it was trash or an animal, sometimes a person or other things; it filled the time as the rain fell.

Pittering.

Plinking on the roof and against the windows.

Drop – drop – drop. Pattering.

"Look. That isn't just trash."

"Holy cat shit," Ben yelled, "it's a boat. It's a friggin boat come to get us." He waved frantically. Everyone pushed forwards to look.

It was a big boat, maybe the size of a yacht with a cover over the deck, windows, and a small life raft, sitting, and tied on the back.

Coral's face went bright with a grin. He was ready to relax to the sound of motor instead of the constant raindrops.

He suddenly stopped smiling.

Where was the sound of the motor?

He was tall enough to see over everyone's heads.

The boat spun lazily, stern first; then, it started coming closer, starboard first. In a second, it swirled again and was bow first. No one was controlling the boat. It swept against the side of the hotel, but had it hit the part with the crumbling foundation, they might have felt the place shake, but instead the boat glanced off, rolled, and went along its way.

"No," a woman slammed herself against the window, "come

get us."

"Hey." A man slammed fists on the glass. "We're here."

Without much noise, the glass cracked and spun out into the water below. Both the woman and man next to it fell out, and because so many had pressed forwards to see, they dropped out of the picture window frame like lemmings. Ben vanished out the window. Sara screamed and grabbed for her husband, Mitch.

He caught her hand and tried to pull her back, but either the couple behind her wanted to jump or was leaning that way; their weight pulled Sara down with them. They all splashed and then screamed as the water surrounded them. Mitch was still leaning out, holding onto the wall and his arm out in the rain.

Mitch yanked his arm back, unsure how his wife could be gone, but his eyes rolled back in his head, and he began to roar and scream, turning his back to the window and going toward the rest. Coral knocked Lydia and Sammy away to safety. Pax shoved Annie behind him, but Mitch was crazed.

Gus drew his gun to shoot, but Mitch was moving too fast; Gus didn't have a clear shot. Katie bounded forwards and slammed into the howling man's midsection, driving him to the floor. Pax and Jake fell on him and yanked out handcuffs and called for rope as they beat him down. He was no longer their friend but a crazed animal.

Katie growled at him.

When Mitch was tied, they left him in the room and closed the door.

"The boat...what about the boat?" Lydia asked.

Coral understood that she was confused after seeing it and thinking for one precious second that they were about to be rescued and taken to safety. She had thought the nightmare was over.

It wasn't.

"That was just a boat, Lydia. No one was running it," Coral said quietly.

"Why don't they come?" Lydia sobbed. "Will they tomorrow? The next day? When will they come for us?"

Sammy held her mother, crying as well, "I wanna go home."

"Me, too," Coral said. For the first time, his eyes filled with tears of frustration and fear.

"Where's Tina?" Marnie asked.

"Oh, Jeez, she was one of those who fell out, wasn't she?" Annie said.

Marnie ran from the room, crying.

"We have enough food for maybe six-seven days, " Dana said happily and noted something in the little notebook she carried around all the time.

"Way to go, Dana. Good thing they fell out the window, huh?" Jake sneered.

"Unless you can survive on barbeque sauce, we're down to the last of things, Jake."

"We'll come up with something." Jake leaned back and thought about food. He was so damned hungry all the time.

"Why the hell are you looking at my dog?" Pax snapped.

Jake shrugged.

"No. Seriously. Why are you looking at Katie that way?"

"Jake," Coral began.

Jake glared, "Just saying that the dog is eating our food, and there comes a time when survival of the fittest rules. We'll have to eat what we can."

Pax exploded and yelled, "You touch my dog, and I will freakin' kill you, you son of a bitch."

Annie touched his arm. "Pax…."

"He wants to eat my dog. Sick bastard."

"Don't touch my cat," said Annie as she whirled on Jake as she thought of that "you leave Blackie alone."

"We aren't gonna eat the animals," Gus said.

"How are you gonna survive then, Gus? You thinking about how maybe the dead are looking tasty?"

"That's sick."

Jake continued, ignoring Annie. "What about Oren or Mitch? They're fresh."

"He's serious. He is. My God, Jake, what comes after the animals and Mitch and Oren? Sammy? Me?" Dana screamed at him.

Lydia clutched Sammy closer to her. "Don't even look at my baby."

Jake urged them to follow him, "Come look at this. I saw this early this morning." He opened a closet, and under the junk at the bottom were cans of food. "Someone hid stuff here. They want more than their share. Who was it?"

Coral looked at every face around him. "It could be anyone here or one of the people who fell."

"It's a lot of extra calories for us," Dana said, picking the can up from the shelf and putting it in a box. "Chili." "This will be good unless you give it all to the dog."

Pax turned on her, "What if I give her half my share? Huh? But no, she gets a full share. She took Mitch out before he could hurt anyone. She did her part. What have you done?"

"She *has* done more than you, Dana," Jake admitted, "did you hide the food?" Dana let the box drop at her feet, took a step, and slapped Jake.

Without thinking, he slapped her back.

"Hey." Gus swung his gun around.

"Stop it," Coral yelled, "everyone stop it." He pointed at Gus. "You stop pointing that thing at people, or I'll take it away, you hear me? And Jake, you knock off the threats. You touch one of the animals or anything, and you'll deal with me. Dana, put the food back, and let Lydia help. None better be missing, and I will guard it myself to keep it safe."

Lydia took Sammy's hand, and she and Dana took the box back with the rest of the food.

"Katie gets a portion. The cat can eat. Stop the infernal fighting."

At dinnertime, Marnie was gone, and so was Mitch; they thought maybe she had helped him, and they had both gone out the window. Dana took a pad and pencil she carried and figured the calories and food with two less people.

Her smile chilled Coral to the core as he watched her add the numbers.

All the medicine, the food, and everything they needed in other stores out there were beneath the water, thirty or forty feet down. Even with flooding, they could have scavenged for things, but with the water being poison, they couldn't touch a thing below the surface. How much was lost below?

Once people would have thought about things they couldn't get to, such as diamonds and gold, fancy electronics, and treasures. Coral dreamed of a tangy, crunchy apple, a salad with juicy tomatoes and crisp lettuce, a tender steak and buttery, salty corn on the cob. It was enough to make him cry, wanting that so badly.

That night, Jake vanished.

Chapter 7

Jake had his own stash of food and a few bottles of rum. When everyone was asleep and the rain had settled from a hard downpour to a light pattering on the roof, he slipped out of his room and crept down the hallway. Most of the rest didn't come near this part of the hotel, the oldest section that had a crumbling foundation and a ceiling that was falling in globs and pieces.

He went into a room.

Sitting on the floor, Jake opened the cans with his knife. He was so hungry, and now he had a can of ravioli, a can of white beans, a pack of baked potato chips, and a big, family-sized can of peaches in thick syrup. After he ate and drank his two cans of orange soda, he drank the syrup and belched.

He felt bad about slapping Dana and being angry to her. He hoped she would accept his apology and thought the can of meatballs and spaghetti-o would help. He felt bad about the way he had treated Pax, too. The last thing Jake would ever do was to harm an animal, much less eat one. He had just been feeling ornery and wanted to pick fights.

Far below, the mud and stone foundation soaked for over a week, shifted.

Jake tried to get to his feet, but as the hotel shifted, a huge beam in the ceiling crashed down through the water-soaked plaster and wood, landing on Jake's back with a loud snap. He flopped onto his side.

He tried to move his legs to get traction but found that his legs, feet, and toes, nothing responded to his attempts to move them. Jake found he couldn't move at all. His arms lay useless by his side. His fifth cervical vertebra was damaged, and had it been a little higher, he wouldn't have been breathing.

He tried to draw in a deep breath and yell for help but was only able to croak out a call that no one could hear.

Rubble surrounded him, and he was partially buried, as were two rooms on his side of the building, along with those that they had avoided because of falling plaster. He didn't know what would become of him now.

Between the cracks and crevices, rain found its way from the roof to the ceiling of the room. Several drops fell across Jake's nose and mouth. For a second he struggled, fearing the water, but then he realized he could give into it and fall into the useless, but pain free nirvana. He allowed himself to relax and accept.

But more drops fell, and he snorted and spit the water out of his nose and mouth. He couldn't breathe with the water filling his breathing passages.

Trying to whip his head aside, he didn't stop the next drops from flooding his breathing. For several seconds, he experienced the pain and horror of drowning, but then everything opened again, and he was able to grab several breaths.

He should be changing by now.

He was supposed to be staring into space, uncaring, unconcerned, and out of pain and fear. But drops followed, and again he chocked; then next, he suffered the painful drowning feelings.

Jake was one of the few who were immune to the rain's effects.

He didn't change and go smooth but lay in the room and suffered natural water boarding torture until he was quite insane.

As the next drops began to fall, Jake watched them, eyes panicked, silently screaming. He screamed a very long time.

Chapter 8

"The floor is a few inches deep now," Coral said. They sat in the lounge area that they also used as a kitchen. The room smelled horrible from unwashed bodies, the rotting dead, and stagnate water. He tried to remember fresh, clean, dry air.

Lydia had given Sammy her own share of food so that the child's stomach wouldn't ache so badly. Sammy only rocked back and forth and cried. The extreme tilt of the hotel didn't amuse her anymore, and the animals had lost their charm. Every day was hunger pangs, damp air, inside stink, and pinging rain on the roof and windows.

Drip. Drop. Ping. Patter. Endless patter.

"Tonight is the night," Lydia said cryptically.

Coral nodded. "Are you sure? Are you sure it needs to be now?"

Dana wrote numbers in her notebook, "Two less. I can take the calories from here and move them...yes...yes, that'll work."

"I'm sure. It's time. Waiting isn't going to give us a different outcome, so I might as well do it tonight. It doesn't matter; Sammy is always hungry now."

"Maybe we could adjust the amount and give her more."

Lydia shook her head, as Dana looked worried about having to move the portions around again. "It worked for Oren, so it'll work for us."

"We had to. We couldn't keep feeding him and caring for him when...you know...he didn't know who we were or he was, and he wasn't even thinking or anything. He was a shell of a man." Coral didn't know why he was talking about it again.

They had voted in favor of giving him the *medicine* and letting him slip away so that they had more food. No one was able to care for him all of the time, and he couldn't do a thing for himself; he didn't eat unless they told him to take each bite.

Coral had handed Oren the cup {*Oh, Socrates, drink this hemlock*}. He had asked Oren to drink it and go to sleep. Oren, following the directions, swallowed every drop of the concoction the others had made. It was a drink with enough random things from the medicine they had left and liquor to knock out a moose, they thought.

Coral sat with Oren until the man nodded off.

Oren's breathing went shallow, and his blood pressure dropped.

After a little while, Pax and Dan helped Coral with Oren's body as they rolled and tied it into a sheet for his shroud. He was given a sea burial as he was lowered into the water that kept rising.

"What will people think? Will they see what we didn't bring here and wonder why we didn't adapt and survive? Will they think we could have done better?"

"What people?"

"The rain will stop, and the water will finally dry up even though it'll take a long time. But they will come looking for more survivors and find that we were here a while."

Pax shook his head, "What people? Coral, where are they?"

"They're in buildings in places…cities…Little Rock. And there will be the military guys, and they'll go to the small places such as this and look for people who adapted and survived. People were on ships. There are people alive."

"Just not here," Pax saidi "It may be a year or more. Can you tell me anyway that we can get out of here and find some supplies? If you can, then let's do it right now. Let's go. Come on, Coral." They had this argument several times a day now.

"I wish I had a big bowl of warm chips and some salsa that would kick my ass. Maybe a cold Corona," Coral dreamed aloud.

"I can't do this anymore," Lydia said, "so, I'll do like Oren did." She went on as if there had been no interruption. "Goodnight. Come on, Sammy."

Annie hugged her, wiping tears away as she did so. Pax and Coral hugged them. When Lydia had said her goodnights to everyone, she took Sammy to their room.

Lydia handed Sammy a glass, and she took a glass; they drank the cocktails, grimacing a little over the bitter taste. They lay down.

"Is it done?" Annie asked. She was openly crying now

against Pax's shoulder as he patted her back.

"Nope," Gus said, "they're both sleeping, but they seem to be kind of okay. Nothing is happening." He checked every thirty minutes.

"And?" Coral asked.

"Sammy is hardly breathing, but Lydia, it isn't happening like Oren."

"We had different stuff for Oren," Coral said. "Are they gonna awake with their minds messed up from this but still alive? God, Dear God, what is going on here? It's not supposed to be like this. Lydia wanted the pain to go away, and she wanted Sammy to quit hurting," he cried with Pax and Annie.

Dan stared out at the night, water dripping in streams, running down the glass.

Dana counted cans of food and wrote in her notebook.

Gus went to check on Lydia and Sammy again. When he returned, his face was pale, and he was clenching his teeth. "There, it's done."

"The pills finally worked?" asked Annie as she wiped her face.

"It's just done. Okay?" Gus gripped the doorframe with one hand and closed his eyes tight for a second. No one asked anything else when he finally sat in a chair and lowered his face to cry into his hands for a long time.

Coral and Pax went in and wrapped Lydia and Sammy together in sheets, ignoring their floppy necks that were obviously broken. They all stood together and let the bodies go into the water.

Six remained.

Chapter 9

On the twelfth day, they lost two more of their group. Dan had a thought to get all the trash they could find and parts of the hotel and to make a boat to sail away on. Everyone watched as he worked on it for days, covering himself in baggies and letting everything dry out. When he was finished with his creation, it was little more than a small tub.

"Put food and other supplies in there after you show me it's sea worthy," Coral told him, "I don't want you doing this."

"We should have all worked on a better one long ago and gotten out of here," Dan said, "give me my share."

"No. If you don't make it, we can use your part of the food and water," Dana said as she scribbled in her notebook again. "I can get another two hundred calories here and then move a hundred to there…."

"I want my share, Coral."

"Fine. Show me it'll float, and you can have it," Coral yelled back.

Pax added, "It's not gonna float, Dan, you idiot. You're gonna go in the water, and there's no sense in taking the food with you."

Dan yanked out one of the Glocks and pointed it at Pax, "Give me my share."

"If you shoot him, then I can take five hundred from there and move it…." Dana wrote feverishly.

"Shut up," Annie screamed at Dana, pushing her down.

Dan used the distraction to leap at Pax who drew the Ruger 10/22 and fired it, hitting Dan in his shoulder. Dan yelped with pain as his shoulder was torn up. Cradling his hurt arm, Dan wrapped the bags and slickers around him tightly, and with the tarp over his head, got into his boat-tub.

Coral angrily pushed him off, taking care to cover himself and to use a boot. Coral flung the wet bag to the side, and they stepped away, watching Dan.

"He pulled a gun on me" Pax said quietly.

"You didn't have a choice. He was trying to take the food

from us," Coral responded, "he is crazy."

"I didn't want to shoot him," Pax said, "but he pulled a gun on me."

"It's okay, Pax," Annie said. She stood beside him, watching Dana sit on the floor where she had pushed her.

The tub swirled out into the water, away from the hotel. Dan had a plan to float away and find a bigger group with better supplies and get them to come save the rest.

Dan was about to be a hero. He thought to go back east, across where the bridge used to be, and then keep going east, always east. In time, he would then hit bigger buildings in a city and find help.

He had to keep the tarp up to keep the tub and himself dry. It was hardly raining now, but he was having a difficult time getting the umbrella engaged and under the tarp to hold it aloft. If he had both arms, he would have been able to handle it, but Pax did something totally unexpected.

Why had the man shot him? Dan only wanted his share of the food. He was afloat without food or water, and if he didn't find help fast, he would be in terrible trouble. He also needed medical aid for his shattered shoulder, too.

It was hurting something fierce.

"He's low, isn't he?" Annie watched the little boat.

"He wasn't that low...yeah...he taking on water," Coral stated, as he watched the tub sink lower, "he's going down."

"Dan," Annie called helplessly.

Dan's boat filled with water. His boots were covered. "You shot me, you bastard," he screamed.

He tried to get the boat under control and back to where the others were. He was going to rip Pax apart for shooting him, and then Coral was next for not giving him his food. Dana, he was sick of her notebook and incessant adding and subtracting. He would kill her, too.

His boat went under.

The rest watched Dan fight the water and then start swimming back to the railing. He would climb out and be there right next to them if he kept coming.

"I told him he would have lost the food," Coral said.

"Yep. He's pretty pissed off. Guess he's mad I shot him."

Coral nodded, "I 'spect so."

Dan was a dozen feet away, swimming with one arm but doing a great job of it as he snarled and growled, swallowing the filthy water as he came back. "Ahhhhhhghhhhhhh," Dan screamed at Pax and Coral.

"He's going to attack as soon as he gets to the railing, and he's wet; we can't let him come back here."

"Nope. I hate to do it. I really don't want to," Pax said.

Coral held a hand out. "Want me to?"

Gus growled with an exasperated sound. "Damn, boys." He grabbed the rifle and raised it. Two shots later, the surface of the water was red-stained, and Dan was gone. In disgust, Gus tossed the rifle into the water and watched it sink. "I've had my fill."

Pax chewed a carrot a long time that evening. He shifted the mashed vegetable around in his mouth and tried to taste all of the flavor. "Give Blackie a little more of the canned milk."

"It has had enough. It had its share."

"Give her my share then," Pax told Dana.

Dana narrowed her eyes and poured the rest of the milk into Blackie's little bowl; the kitten purred delightfully. Pax closed his eyes and then reached forward to lay one hand on Blackie's side so that he could not just hear the purring but also feel it. He took Annie's hand and put her hand there on Blackie's side.

Annie smiled and the world lit up for Pax.

"I want them to be okay," Pax said, now leaning into Katie's fur and rubbing his face along her muzzle; she licked him sideways and seemed to be grinning. Annie had brushed her for hours, and Katie's fur shined and gleamed. "Who is a good Katie?"

She woofed.

"What are you doing?" Gus called out to Dana.

"Leave me alone. There's a can under that junk. I think the can has tomato soup."

"Under all that?" Gus asked.

"I can get it. I just have to get over there and crawl down. Do you know how many calories that would add?"

Gus snorted, "No, Do you?"

Dana snapped back as she struggled over a pile of jagged glass, 3.14.

"Get out of that," Coral said.

Dana kept climbing. At the top of the junk, she slid to the right. A sting on her leg made her squeak, and another few bee stings on an arm hurt, but then she was past the glass.

"Oh." Dana looked at her arm. Shards had gone in deeply, and as Dana removed each, blood poured out in rivers. It shouldn't have been taken out unless someone was ready with surgery.

"Let's get something, and we'll get you out, Dana. Be still. Can you catch some sheets and use them to bind those?" Coral asked. He didn't like all the blood seeping out of Dana's arm. Tossing strips to her, he watched her mind him and bind her arm wounds. She raised the injured arm in victory.

"She's a nut," Gus declared.

"She's a nut who may have found some soup; imagine that tonight," Coral said. His eyes were glazed as he was thinking of tangy tomato soup.

"Catch, I found the mother-load," Dana called to them. She used her good arm to toss cans. A can of tomato soup went flying to Coral who cheered. A can of pineapples went to Gus who used both hands to grab it. "Here, Coral." He caught a can of chicken gravy.

He was salivating.

The area Dana was in had fallen apart. Trees had battered into the corner, the roof had leaked, and the old wood split when the foundation shifted, so Dana was in the midst of glass, jagged boards, beams, fallen plaster, and broken furniture and walls.

Cans of food had rolled over sometime, and she was grabbing it all. A small can of green chilies went flying, a can of stewed tomatoes, three old, stale pastries, a can of chicken and dumplings, and finally, a box of macaroni and cheese that wasn't too beat up. "What we have now is 3.141592635. Rain, rain go away, 3.14," Dana muttered to herself.

"I have frogs in my bugles," Pax responded.

"Spaghetti in my cake," Coral quipped, remembering how a thousand years ago, a man named Ed had killed his family in Coral's diner and talked crazy. It had been forever ago.

Dana used a piece of cloth and tied her notebook to a plastic packet that looked like a pastry mix for pizza crust or a muffin mix. She tossed it close to the rubble. "That's mine." She needed both hands to crawl back onto the big pile of junk.

"Your leg."

Dana frowned and looked down. One of her legs was awash in blood. A shard had gotten her, right near her female privates on her thigh. Blood was really pouring.

Dizzy. Dana leaned against a board. She had to climb up and out. She was freezing cold all over and tired. Maybe if she rested a second. She rarely cut herself or anything before, but when she had, she knew she bled badly, and someone had said that could be serious. It was more rare in females than in males, but she was almost a hemophiliac.

Dana couldn't really feel her body anymore. She slumped to the bottom of a pile of rubble, smacking her head on a brick and scraping her neck on a rough, broken board.

"Bled out. Wow," Gus said. He collected the bag and the little notebook tied to it. Throwing the notebook to Annie, Gus added the packet. {It was blueberry pancake/muffin mix} to the rest of what Dana had tossed over. "I want that, looks good. Mmmm Gravy. Nice catch, Coral."

Annie opened the notebook, curiously.

3.14159 26535 89793 stop raining: creamed corn, 23846 26433 83279 stop raining: pinto beans, 50288 pasta, 41971 69399 rain, rain go away, 37510 58209 come again no other day 74944 59230 stop raining, 78164 06286 stop raining 20899 86280, chili beans stop raining, 34211 70679.

"She wasn't all there," Annie said, holding out the notebook.

"I want some of the blueberry mix, too," Pax said. "Can we make the tomato soup tonight, Coral?"

"I think that's a fine idea."

"Oh, add the stewed tomatoes in it. It'll go further and be good." Annie wiped her chin where she drooled. She was so hungry.

She hugged Katie.

Annie pretended she was rubbing the dog and petting her, but deep in her mind, she was figuring how much fat the dog had on her.

Chapter 10

"Make sure I can't see you if I look back," Gus said.

That was all he said. During the mid-day meal, Gus refused food, sharing his portion instead. He didn't say much. He just sat and drank a bottle of whiskey, sipping it, and enjoying the burn. No one knew what he had in mind because he wouldn't elaborate; he just said he would be leaving soon as if a spacecraft might appear and take him away.

They heard a splash and peeked out the glass to see what Gus was doing.

He didn't look around, so the alcohol or their hiding had kept him from coming back and attacking. Coral said that Gus was a fantastic swimmer and when he was younger, he had even dreamed of the Olympics and had done some type of training for it.

"What's he doing?" Annie whispered.

"Swimming. He is swimming, Annie, just swimming."

"Where's he going?"

"That way. He's swimming that way," Coral said.

Gus found a rhythm and swam easily. As far as the eye could see, there was nothing, no land, not a place to go. They watched Gus until he was a tiny dot in the water. They watched until he was gone.

Chapter 11

On the fifteenth day, a bloated sheep swirled by on the current, and they watched it float away. *"Bah, bah, black sheep,"* Annie whispered, petting Blackie. The kitten purred, and Annie tickled and rubbed her ears.

Pax kissed Annie as she lay there on the bed, drowsing. Coral sat across the room in a chair, his feet up, and Katie, even as big as she was, lying across him, her muzzle on his shoulder.

"Have you any wool?" asked Pax as he smiled.

"Yes, sir, yes, sir, three bags full."

Pax put the Glock against her head and pulled the trigger.

"I love you Annie," he whispered. Katie and Blackie had jumped in terror and flew from the room, their nails skittering as they ran away.

Pax figured neither would trust him or want to be around him for a while. They knew he caused the noise.

They knew he took away Annie.

Pax wailed and held his head down, setting the muzzle of the Glock against his jaw line. "Annie…."

He didn't pull the trigger but wailed harder. "I want to feel it. Even if it's horrible, I want to feel it. I want my memories, no matter how bad they are."

"Pull it, Pax," Coral said, "do it."

Pax screamed.

Then he leaned back. He looked at Annie's broken head, forced himself to take it all in and to really see what the bullet had done. "Which is better, Coral?

Tell me the answer. Is it better to have all this pain and fear but also the memories and the part of me that is *me*? I have the part that loves Annie, and she's alive in that memory and happy, laughing. I know who you are. I don't want to kill you. You're my friend."

"Yeah."

"I'll go away."

"So will the pain. And the fear," Coral told him, "let it go."

Pax stared into the Glock's barrel again. "Who will keep the memories?"

"Me, I'll keep them all."

"All alone? All alone," Pax said, "it's better to go *smooth*, Coral. I wanna be smooth."

Coral jumped at the noise; the Glock was loud in the room.

In a while, Coral tossed the Glock into the water in the main stairwell and went to another room. Katie and Blackie joined him.

Chapter 12

On the seventeenth day, Coral watched the water. It wasn't raining as hard, but it was still sprinkling; it always was.
Blackie and Katie chased the red ball.
On the horizon, a boat-shape formed, coming closer.
Coral heard the drone of a motor.
He sat and stared into nothing.

(Fort Worth 2013)

Made in United States
Orlando, FL
26 May 2024